Tempted
BY THE JAGUAR

RIVERFORD SHIFTERS BOOK ONE

CRISTINA RAYNE

Fantastical Press

Dragon Shifters of Elysia

Where Sleeping Dragons Lie

When Fire Dragons Fall *coming July 2018

The Vampire Underground

Tales from the Vampire Underground Anthology

A Whisper in the Darkness *coming 2018

Incarnations of Myth

Seeking the Oni

Falling for Enma *coming Fall 2018

Fractured Multiverse

(Writing as C.G. Garcia)

The Supreme Moment: Kairos

The Supreme Moment: Externus *coming Fall 2018

Black Crimson *coming 2019

The Golden Mage Trilogy

The Kingdom of Eternal Sorrow

The Man Within the Temple

The Last Stone Cast

Dedicated to my sister, Rachel,
who is one of my biggest fans

CHAPTER 1

ylie Moore pulled her backpack from the backseat of her car and was in the process of straightening when she heard it, the soft scrape of a shoe slipping slightly on some loose gravel somewhere in the parking lot behind her. Freezing instinctually, she started to turn just as the back of her head was roughly pushed forward, and her temple slammed against the top of the doorframe. For one endless moment, it felt as though her entire skull had shattered as the inky blackness of the night exploded in a flash of white-hot pain across her vision.

Her backpack and keys fell from fingers gone slack from shock, and Kylie staggered back a step, blinded by pain and her mind a swirl of confusion. A sense of vertigo hit her as her world tilted sideways, only to feel the side of her body hit the pavement hard a second later.

A cry was torn from her lips as the sudden jolt caused what felt like a dozen knives to stab into her head. Then hands grabbed her arms and yanked them away from where she had been cradling her head, and her watery vision darkened almost completely in a sudden wash of pain as someone began dragging her along the asphalt away from her car, her body as limp and unresponsive as a ragdoll's.

Dazed thoughts of being carjacked melted into panicked, disjointed thoughts that, no, something much worse was happening, and Kylie tried to struggle. However, her consciousness was fading fast, and she just couldn't seem to make her body do *anything*.

Then her head banged into the edge of something hard…and the next thing Kylie knew, she found herself folded up into a very uncomfortable semblance of a fetal position, her hands stuck up behind her neck. She tried to flex her fingers, but both hands felt dead, as though she had been lying on them for quite some time.

It was pitch black, the air smelling heavily of motor oil and something rotten and sickly as though she was lying next to either a garbage can or a pile of vomit. The floor beneath her body vibrated, and a slight roaring filled her ears. Both the back of her head and one of her temples was throbbing something fierce, and she couldn't help the small moan that fell from her lips.

What the hell was going on? Her head pounding, confusion, her mouth dry—it was as if she had just woken up in the weirdest place ever with the worst hangover in existence. Only, she didn't drink.

Kylie tried to move both her arms and legs, trying to remember what she had been doing. She'd had a study group for genetics class today. She was sure she had left the university library; she could remember getting into her car and driving off towards the freeway with the intention of going back to her apartment. Then...then...

Something rough and sturdy painfully dug into her bare ankles and upper thighs simultaneously as she tried to straighten her legs, and her wrists met that same barrier as she tried to bring her arms down from her head. It was only then that the fogginess of her mind suddenly evaporated into terror. She was freaking *tied up*!

Now in a panic, Kylie yanked her wrists hard against what she now knew to be coils of rope and nearly choked as the sharp movement caused an unnoticed cord of rope to tighten around her neck. Rather than just tied together, a length of rope had also been connected to the bindings around her wrists and then wrapped around her neck, ensuring that any pulling on her part would only lead to strangling herself.

She frantically thrashed her body around in an effort to free her legs, but the thick rope cut painfully into her skin and only seemed to tighten. Whoever had tied her up had done their job extremely well.

In some remote part of her mind not yet touched by hysteria, Kylie desperately hoped that this was just some cruel, horribly misguided prank someone was playing on her while the more practical part of her brain was screaming that she was in shit so deep she was already drowning. Someone *had* to have hit her over the head. Her temple throbbed too sharply to attribute it to even a migraine.

A memory surfaced, one she wished she didn't know. For the past year, half a dozen women had gone missing from various places within the city, even a freshman from her own university. No bodies, no clues from security footage or witnesses, *nothing* was ever found of them again, as though they had all literally vanished from the face of the earth. The last one had vanished a couple of months ago.

No—not a couple of months, today *if I don't figure out how to get the hell out of here!*

Kylie managed to roll her body to the left but immediately hit a barrier. After a bit of a struggle, she succeeded in rolling herself in the other direction only to promptly roll onto what felt like a shovel. She froze even though the metal edge was digging uncomfortably into her shoulders, on the verge of a full-on panic attack. The vibrating floor and the smells now made horrifying sense. She was in the freaking trunk of a car!

She began to struggle and strain against her bindings with a frenzied effort, nearly biting through her tongue in an attempt to keep the anguished wails of terror at bay. It was evident she had been knocked out at some point, and even though her mouth had not been covered, there was no way she was about to possibly alert her abductor that she was now awake.

They were probably driving on a freeway or high-way, so there was little to no chance that anyone would be able to hear her screaming above the normal rumble of travel and passing cars. She had no idea how long she had even been unconscious. Her only chance would be to either free herself before the monster, or monsters, opened the trunk, or if failing that, screaming her lungs out when the car stopped.

Her wrists burned as she strained, but her abductor had left almost no wiggle room. The ropes might as well have been zip ties for all the progress she had made. By now her hands were so dead she couldn't even wiggle her fingers, and her legs were screaming with pain.

It was no use.

Kylie fell limp and clenched her jaw against the sob of despair that wanted to break loose. There was a very good chance that she was about to die that day, and damned if she was going to give the bastard the satisfaction of seeing her tears, the fear that was threatening to choke the breath from her. She had to save her strength, keep her mind as clear as her throbbing headache allowed, her eyes sharp. She took a long, shuddering breath, trying not to gag on the smells that were coming from the trunk's carpet, trying to calm the pounding of her heart that sounded as loud as gunfire in her ears.

By the time the car started to slow down, Kylie felt as though she had been trapped in that trunk for days. She had debated back and forth on whether or not to pretend to still be unconscious or to try screaming the moment the car stopped, and now that the moment of truth was almost here, Kylie's panic returned with a vengeance. What if she screamed and that was the thing that doomed her? What if she kept her eyes closed, pretended to still be unconscious, and she missed seeing the only chance to escape she would get?

The moment the car came to a complete stop, something in Kylie snapped, and she was screaming for help before she even realized that she was going to do it. Bellowing at the top of her lungs, she managed a dozen "help me's" before the trunk was wrenched open and three more after before a large, dark figure abruptly filled her vision. An equally large, sweaty and calloused hand roughly slapped over her mouth mid-scream.

Kylie instinctually tried to bite at the hand. However, it lifted before she could really sink her teeth into anything, and a second later her mouth exploded with pain as that same hand backhanded her with brutal force before she could even think to scream again. She felt the soft tissue of her bottom lip slice across the sharp edges of her teeth, and a trickle of hot blood began to flow into her mouth.

She only had just enough time to suck in a shocked breath before she was wrenched out of the trunk by her shoulders and promptly dumped face-first onto the ground into a cluster of tall weeds, jarring her head and causing pain like a knife stabbing into her skull to shoot through her temple. Kylie gritted her teeth and immediately forced her body to roll onto its side.

"Somebody! *Help me*!" she screamed over and over as soon as her face was free of the weeds even though the only things she could see were darkness and the dark silhouette of dozens of trees.

It was hopeless. Now that she had seen the trees and knew that he had brought her into the forest that surrounded Riverford, a forest that went on for miles in all directions, it was pretty much game over for her. Yet, she just couldn't make herself stop crying out for help. She couldn't give up on the slim hope that someone else just might be nearby, just might be able to hear her screams, because dammit! She couldn't die now! She couldn't die without ever knowing what had happened to her parents! Hadn't fate shit on Paul and her enough!

So Kylie screamed and screamed and writhed within her bindings, probably doing terrible damage to her legs and wrists as she strained to break the ropes, but not even her anger and desperation was enough to free her. It was only after she had screamed her voice to almost nonexistence that she realized that her abductor was standing only a foot away from her head, just—standing there with his head down, watching her futile struggles.

There was no moon that night so even her dark-adjusted eyes couldn't make out more than the outline of his body. He was tall, looming over her still and quiet like one of the phantom trees surrounding them. Was he smiling? Smirking? Or worse, did he have no expression at all? The thought of her possibly giving him exactly the show that he wanted made Kylie immediately stop her thrashing.

For the space of what felt like an eternity, the only sound was the rustle of the wind flowing through the multitudes of tree branches and her ragged breathing.

That he hadn't said one word to her was more terrifying than if he had been reciting a list of horrible things he was about to do to her.

Kylie told herself she wouldn't scream, that she wouldn't move until she saw an opening. Tied up the way she was, he had only left her two possible weapons. Now that one of them, her voice, had obviously failed to bring her help, she had only one possible, one very *sharp* way out of this as her cut lip and the taste of blood in her mouth could attest. He only had to get close to her, or more specifically his *neck*, in just the right position. One tiny hope; one try.

She had to wait; she had to stay sharp. Kylie could almost hear her father whispering those words to her again, words that she had lived by, that she had clung to as her anchor for the past twelve years.

However, when he sank down onto one knee and she saw the large pair of metal scissors moving towards her stomach, Kylie couldn't help flinching with a small cry of alarm. Her abductor's free hand shot out of the darkness to wrap around her neck, squeezing with just enough pressure for her to feel the rope coiled around her neck begin to bite into her delicate flesh but not enough to strangle. A warning.

He was now close enough to her that she could see the whites of his eyes, could see him staring directly at her with unblinking dark eyes that sent a shiver up her spine. There was nothing human in that gaze, nothing even remotely resembling an emotion. Just what kind of monster was she at the mercy of?

Without moving his gaze from her face, he began to slowly cut away at the hem of her blouse. Kylie lay frozen on her side, afraid to move, afraid to even breathe as she felt the cold metal of the scissors brush against her skin as they slowly moved up her abdomen.

It was in those dead eyes. She could see it as plainly as if he had announced it. He would not be satisfied with just cutting all her clothes off. He wouldn't be satisfied because he had never intended to violate her body in the way she had feared. No, this was a monster the likes of which she could have never imagined.

Kylie could feel a scream welling up in her throat. In a second or two it would break free and with it, very likely her sanity. Kylie opened her mouth, and a sound emerged that she had never heard come from a human throat, a long, drawn-out keening of pure despair that seemed to come directly from her soul.

...and something deep within her entire being shattered.

CHAPTER 2

A wave of what felt like the biggest muscle spasm she had ever had washed through Kylie's entire body a split-second before every inch of her began to contract and expand as though she was a balloon being inflated to the brink of bursting. For a painful beat, the ropes around her wrists, neck, ankles, and thighs cut excruciatingly into her flesh before inexplicably snapping as though they were made of straw. Her strange keening also began to change in pitch, to expand until the roar of an apex predator filled the once eerily silent night.

Rage, fear, and a sense of blood lust filled her mind. An enemy was here! An enemy was hurting her! With a deafening roar, Kylie lunged at the figure that had fallen back onto his ass, that was frantically trying to scoot away from her. She could now see him as clearly as though it were twilight. She felt huge; she felt powerful as two large paws of golden, black-spotted fur slammed onto his chest, claws sinking past layers of cloth that felt as flimsy as silk and tearing into that soft, soft flesh as her enemy was flattened to the ground with a shriek of pain.

The coppery smell of blood and another acrid scent of something she had never smelled before filled her nostrils, and the rage that saturated her every pore instantly doubled until all she could think about, all she wanted was the taste of that blood on her tongue. She opened her jaws wide and went for her attacker's throat just as what felt like a battering ram hit her squarely on the side, causing Kylie to tumble uncontrollably off the bleeding body until she landed in a heap on her side.

With a roar, she scrambled onto all fours, hunching low into a defensive stance and her tail lashing sharply like the crack of a whip behind her. Her mind was so lost to the rage, to the fear of being attacked that she didn't even stop to wonder why she was on all fours, that she roared, or that she actually had a *tail* to lash behind her. Her entire world had narrowed down to the large spotted feline standing challengingly between her and her prey that was currently staggering off into the protection of the trees, its eyes flashing with a bit of night shine as it stared her down but did not try to move closer.

Kylie lashed out at the much larger great cat, swatting at the air between them warningly with her claws, before backing up a couple of steps and resuming her defensive stance with a series of sharp chuffs. That was *her* prey! How dare the other, one of her own *brethren*, try to take it from her!

She let out another angry chuff and clawed the ground. The other cat blinked its large eyes and then tilted its head in a manner that her senses were screaming was utterly *wrong*—unnatural.

Slowly it sat back onto its haunches and then before her alarmed eyes, the spotted cat's entire body began to ripple in an utterly unsettling way before the mass of its body began to shrink down and rearrange itself. Spotted fur rapidly melted into smooth, human skin until everything settled and the body of a man crouched in its place.

Her mind in its current state just could not comprehend what it had just seen. A naked, black-haired man now crouched before her, but he still smelled the same. He still smelled like the great cat of before.

The man stared back at her warily, moving to sit with his knees bent up, and then he carefully rested his arms onto them.

"It's all right," he said softly in a deep, nonthreatening voice. "Be calm. Be calm. I'm not angry. I'm not going to hurt you."

Kylie snarled at him and took a cautious step back. What was he saying? He attacked her! He let her prey escape!

"You're okay," he cooed in that same, soft voice. "There's no danger here. I just want to help you. Will you let me help you?"

Help her? Some of her rage subsided as utter confusion began to creep into her mind. What had just happened here?

"Can you shift back now? So we can talk?" the man asked, his eyes wide and imploring.

Kylie paused in the process of baring her teeth, the word "shift" tickling the edges of a distant memory even as a surge of fear washed over her, effectively snuffing out the uncontrollable rage of before. It was *him*, she realized suddenly, this stranger who had turned from cat to man before her very eyes. It was him she was afraid of, afraid that he was going to find out about—

—that I'm a—

Her eyes flickered down to the ground, to her two spotted paws with claws fully extended and the fur matted with blood, and she abruptly let out a sound of dismay that did not at all sound like something that should have come out of any kind of feline's throat.

Shit! I'm a jaguar! Kylie suddenly screeched in utter shock within her mind, a mind that was now once again completely her own. She scrambled back in a panic until her rump hit a tree, looking with horror at the unknown naked man who had suddenly jumped to his feet.

He saw! He saw!

"No—don't—!" he exclaimed, taking a step towards her, but she didn't wait to hear the rest.

Kylie bounded off into the night, running as though the Devil, himself, was on her heels, dodging trees and brush and jumping over exposed roots with an almost preternatural grace even as her mind was in full-blown freak-out mode. She had *shifted*! Another shifter had *seen* her! How had this happened?

Like a mantra, those thoughts ran through her mind over and over as she raced through the dense forest with no destination in mind except *away*. She ran as fast as she could even though she couldn't tell if he was following her, couldn't tell if his scent was among the thousand different scents that she drew in as she panted. The assault of unknown smells almost overwhelmed her, fueled her fear and panic, and Kylie had no idea how to separate herself from it.

So she just ran until she could hear the hum of

various vehicles zooming down what she hoped was the east highway out of Riverford and could see the faint flashes of their headlights through the trees as they drove past. By now, her breathing had become severely labored, and various muscles were beginning to scream with pain in places she was not used to.

She slowed down to a more manageable pace and turned west to run parallel to the road but still well hidden by the trees and the darkness. *I have to get home! I have to call Paul!*

Never mind that she had been attacked and abducted by what was probably a serial killer or that she had been seconds away from ripping out his throat. The only thing that mattered now, that *could* matter, was that she had *shifted* and had been seen by another shifter.

She had to get to Paul. He was the only chance she had now.

CHAPTER 3

Kylie dashed across the highway and back into the cover of the forest, making it across before any more cars managed to come around the bend. The way her heart pounded within the chest of her new form felt utterly unfamiliar and scary, but she knew now was not the time to freak out about it. She had no way of knowing if she had managed to lose the black-haired man back there in the forest, or if he had even decided to give chase in the first place. She would have plenty of time to fall apart once she made it back to the relative safety of her apartment.

This area was thankfully familiar. The road was definitely the east highway out of Riverford. She moved through the trees as fast as her waning strength could sustain, heading north along the perimeter of the city towards a children's neighborhood park that skated along the edges of the forest. It was only a few blocks from her apartment complex.

It was still the dead of night, so hopefully no one would be out to see the large jaguar moving through the shadows. Being shot by a frightened neighbor on top of everything else she had already endured that night would just be the rotten cherry on top of a sundae gone sour.

By the time she reached the park, Kylie's entire body was trembling with exhaustion. She was unable to even prevent her tongue from hanging out of her mouth as she panted. Her bones also ached in a strange way that made her feel as though she had injured them somehow and they were dangerously on the verge of shattering. Even so, she only paused long enough behind one of the trees along the edge to take in a few deep, wheezing breaths while her eyes swept the length of the park within her field of vision, looking for any signs of movement among all the swing sets, slides, and jungle gyms.

Only when she was satisfied that section of the park was empty did Kylie shoot out from the cover of the trees as though she had been fired from a cannon and raced across the grass to the street and the first apartment building to the right. Keeping to the shadows, she slunk along the building to an alleyway that she hoped would offer her more protection than moving through the residential streets.

As Kylie bounded down the alley, her once sharp vision began to blur, and she could no longer see the far end of the dark alley as clearly. Then something that felt like the worst muscle spasm she had ever had rolled across her entire body, starting from her shoulder to the tip of her tail, causing her to stumble and fall onto her belly just when she emerged from the alley into the street.

For one, panic-filled moment, Kylie couldn't get up, all four limbs shaking as though she was starting to seize. Shit! Was she starting to shift back?

"Whoa! What the hell!" a young male voice suddenly yelped, causing Kylie to instinctually turn her head and snarl in the direction of the voice.

A surge of adrenaline shot through her veins, and Kylie was instantly back on all fours before she had even made the decision to move, crouching defensively as a pair of teenaged boys stood frozen along the curb of the street a mere five feet away. That same acrid scent she had smelled after she had attacked her abductor back in the forest filled the air, and it was then that Kylie understood what it was she smelled.

Fear. Pungent and sharp and exciting, it was not a sweet scent, or even a meaty, organic scent. The scent of fear did not even remotely resemble anything she had ever smelled as a human. The aroma was almost an emotion, one that the feline part of her understood *very* well.

It was then that the urge to lunge at the two boys nearly overwhelmed her. Only the small part of her that was still completely human, the part that realized the horror of what she was on the brink of doing, managed to turn her body just as she started to pounce on the nearest boy who had suddenly become prey and sprang off in the opposite direction instead. With her own fear and disgust spurring her on, Kylie ran down the street with a renewed vigor, her control hanging by a thread.

She had to get home. She had to get home before she accidentally ran into someone else because she wasn't so sure she would have the strength of mind to run away a second time. That fear drove her down street after street at a speed she should not have been capable of as exhausted as she was, a large shadow just a bit lighter than the surrounding night that could very easily be mistaken for a large dog to anyone who may have caught a glimpse of her.

At the first sight of her apartment building, Kylie couldn't help the whine of relief that burst out from deep within her throat. Her vision was already losing its feline acuity, and the strange spasms of before were once again spreading across her body. She made it a few feet across the parking lot before her body simply collapsed mid-lope. She fell onto her side, and her body began to violently seize, causing her to accidentally bite down hard on her lolling tongue. The salty, coppery taste of blood filled her mouth as she felt various parts of her body tighten, then stretch until she felt as though her muscles were about to tear.

Kylie opened her mouth to roar, but a very human cry of pain shattered the silence instead. Startled, she opened tear-filled eyes and saw her once again human hand, her fingers stained dark, lying on the asphalt near her face. She shuddered, with both the chill of the night air and the lingering spasms that still rocked her body and drew in an equally shaky breath. However, when she tried to lift her head, a wave of utter exhaustion washed through her body so powerfully, so heavy, that for a few terrifying moments, it was almost too much effort to breathe.

Fighting off panic, Kylie forced herself to relax completely and concentrate on merely breathing, trying not to think of the utter mortification she would feel if she passed out right then and there and someone stumbled upon her naked, unconscious body in the morning. However, instead of going away, her exhaustion only seemed to be getting worse and her eyelids heavier.

Kylie realized being found naked was exactly what was about to happen if she didn't somehow manage to drag her butt over to her parking space where she prayed to everything holy her car, and more importantly her backpack with her key to the apartment, would be. She still only had vague memories of her head being bashed against the doorframe of her car, but she wasn't altogether sure it had happened here in this parking lot.

She gritted her teeth and forced herself to roll over onto her stomach. Then drawing a deep, steadying breath, she managed to climb onto her knees even though it felt as if someone had dropped a hundred pound weight onto her back. How ironic that she was now forced to move on all fours while in her human form.

It was slow going, but Kylie finally made it to the end of the lot without incident and literally felt tears well up in her eyes when she saw her little black sedan parked next to her neighbors' SUV. At least now she knew where she had been attacked.

Thoughts of her attacker, of the pain of the rope cutting deeply into her flesh, suddenly flooded her mind, and Kylie viciously cut off that line of thinking. She couldn't handle any of that right now. She would fall apart, and she could *not* allow that to happen again, especially out in the open like this. Losing it had already caused her to involuntarily shift. What if it happened again and some of her neighbors happened to stumble on her?

Maybe the universe finally decided to take pity on her because as Kylie dragged herself between the two vehicles, her eyes immediately caught sight of her keys just a little ways beneath her car. She had been afraid that they had been lost somewhere in the trunk from hell she had awakened in, and seeing them there lifted just a little bit of the enormous weight on her back, enough that she was able to force herself upright onto her knees on the first try.

Please let it be there...

Kylie tugged on the handle of the rear driver's side door and found it unlocked. On the floorboard was the item she sought. Leaning farther into the car, she grabbed her backpack and unzipped the small pouch in the front. Pulling out her cell phone was like finding the prize after running a marathon.

She could finally call Paul. He would know what to do.

Her windows were tinted pretty dark. It would probably be okay for her to hunker down in the backseat of her car for the twenty or thirty minutes it would take him to drive to her apartment because she really didn't think she had the strength to make it to her door, even though her apartment was on the first floor.

Using the last dregs of her strength, she thrust herself onto the backseat in a sort of dive, pulling the door closed after she had wiggled around and was situated. Just that simple exertion caused her head to swim and her breathing to become as labored as though she had been running for hours. Her energy reserves were nearly completely depleted. How long before her body just said "screw it" and just shut down? Skipping dinner today was seriously coming back to bite her in the ass.

Kylie took a couple of deep, calming breaths and quickly turned her phone on to call Paul. After the fourth ring, a bit of panic began to surface. Had he forgotten his cell phone in his office again? Like her, he did not have a landline, his reasoning being that he was seldom home. If she managed to survive this horrendous night, then maybe they should both rethink the matter.

On the fifth ring, the phone went to his voice mail, and Kylie hung up with a curse. Leaving him a message was absolutely out of the question. She slowly turned towards the apartment building with a look of despair. She wasn't sure she could make it to the building, much less her apartment. She looked down at her phone. Did she dare call one of her friends? But—how in the hell would she even begin to explain what she was doing sitting in her back seat naked and seconds away from passing out.

No. No one except Paul could know *anything* had happened to her at all. It was too dangerous. It was also too dangerous to stay in the car. If she passed out and someone found her before she managed to get a hold of Paul…

Her phone's ringtone suddenly went off, nearly scaring her half to death, the sudden adrenaline surge making her chest constrict painfully. For a couple of seconds, Kylie had to fight off the blackness that had begun to enter the edges of her vision before she was able to clumsily tap the "talk" button on her phone and bring it up to her ear. For a split-second, she had a momentary panic when she realized that she had answered before checking to see who was calling, but then a familiar deep voice said her name anxiously, and relief like she had never felt washed through her like a balm.

"Paul…" she said, her voice cracking as she very nearly lost her hard-fought battle against her threatening tears.

"What happened? Are you hurt?" Paul demanded, fear making his voice sound deeper than normal.

"I can't—can you please come to my apartment?"

Kylie pleaded, hating how young and pathetic she sounded. Now was not the time to fall apart, dammit! "Too much has happened. Just please come."

"Kylie…" Paul replied, sounding anguished. "I'm not in Riverford. I'm in Dallas for the conference, remember?"

Her heart instantly sank. She *had* forgotten. Kylie glanced at the clock on her phone. Ten after five. It was much later in the morning than she had thought. Even by plane, he was at least a little over an hour away. It would take a miracle for him to reach her in less than two, and by then, probably three-fourths of her apartment complex would be heading to the parking lot for work or school. There was no way she wouldn't be seen before Paul could get to her.

"Paul—I *shifted*," Kylie told him urgently.

She could practically hear his shock in the sudden silence on the other end. "Did someone see you?" he demanded, the fear even more blatant in his tone.

"Yes," she admitted in a small voice.

"Another shifter or a human?"

"Both."

"Where are you now?"

"I'm in my car in the parking lot of my apartment building."

"Why are you still—no there's no time. Listen to me,

Kylie. Get inside your apartment, and turn your phone off. Don't call *anyone*. Don't answer the door unless you hear me say the secret word. I would tell you to destroy your phone, but not having one would be worse. I'll be there as soon as humanly possible."

Kylie glanced out the window and zeroed in on the faraway door of her apartment that was, at the most, the length of a football field away but might as well have been miles. Why oh why did she have to live in a complex where the parking was all the way in the back for everyone? Nevertheless—there were no if ands or buts about it. She would just have to make it on her own. Paul was on his way. She would have to draw strength from that thought alone.

"I'll be waiting," she said with as much determination as she could muster before hanging up immediately, sure she would start crying if she heard his voice again.

There was no use adding to his worries just yet. Kylie had a feeling everything would come crashing down soon enough.

Kylie wasn't sure how, but after at least thirty minutes of alternating between short spurts of dragging herself and pausing to fight off the darkness that was threatening to overwhelm her mind, the door to her apartment was finally before her. She let out a sound that was half-sob, half-laugh. For one terrifying moment, she had very nearly teetered over the knife-thin ledge she had been moving along into unconsciousness halfway there, but by some miracle, she had managed to hold onto consciousness by the skin of her teeth.

The level of exhaustion that she was currently feeling was unlike anything she had ever experienced. She was sure that she had just scraped her knees and elbows raw, but she was so tired that the only thing she could feel was a bone-deep numbness. By sheer force of will, Kylie forced herself to her knees and leaned against the door as she struggled to slide the key into the lock.

After what felt like an eternity of fumbling, she finally managed to get the door open and promptly fell across the threshold with a weak grunt as she landed face-first onto the carpet of her living room. The world was quickly fading fast, but Kylie shook her head in an effort to clear the haziness that had started to creep in and struggled to pull herself the rest of the way inside.

Her hand moved on autopilot to close the door, and her last thought before her mind lost the battle with consciousness was that she hadn't locked the door.

CHAPTER 4

*L*oud pounding sounded right next to her ear, and Kylie's eyes flew open, her heart practically tearing out of her chest. It had taken a couple of seconds before the room blurred into focus, and with some confusion, she realized that she was lying down on the carpet near the front door.

What in the—

A series of rapid, loud raps on the front door made her jump a second time, and Kylie scrambled onto her knees, nearly face-planting on the floor when the world suddenly did a one-eighty. She squeezed her eyes closed with a groan and grabbed her head between her hands, the unexpected vertigo making her feel queasy. It was then, her head bent down as she slowly opened her eyes again, that she noticed that she didn't have a stitch on.

"Shit!" Kylie cried as she scrambled unsteadily to her feet, memories of last night's horrors finally beginning to rise out of the confusion of her still sleep-fogged mind.

That was probably Paul at the door!

Kylie started to turn, intent on going to her bedroom to throw on some clothes when she froze. No—it couldn't be Paul. She hadn't heard him say it. The secret word.

She only had time to take an alarmed step back before the knob started to turn. Shit! The door wasn't locked!

Kylie dashed forward and slammed both hands against the door as hard as she could just as it started to open. However, the door was pushed heavily from the other side, and whoever was standing there managed to wedge a white-sneakered foot into the crack that had momentarily opened. With a cry of terror, she shoved at the door with all her might, but it was as though she was trying to move a brick wall for all the door budged.

"I just want to talk," a vaguely familiar male voice said, sounding much too calm given the battle of force they were engaged in.

"You have the wrong apartment!" Kylie said through gritted teeth. She was still feeling incredibly weak from her ordeal last night and could feel that she was just seconds away from losing the battle.

The guy snorted. "We both know that isn't true," he said, sounding rather matter-of-fact. "I can *smell* you."

His odd words gave her pause only for a split-second, but it was the edge he needed to finally push the door open wide enough for him to squeeze through. In a panic, rather than make a break for her bedroom, Kylie grabbed the doorknob and pulled the door flush against her front and scrambled back until her back hit the wall, using the door to cover her nudity.

Immediately she felt a tug on the door, and Kylie gripped the doorknob so tightly that her entire hand was beginning to hurt. "No! Don't!" she moaned desperately.

The stranger abruptly stopped trying to pull the door away from her.

"I'm not going to hurt you," he said softly.

Kylie sucked in a sharp breath. Those words, that tone—she had heard them before, just last night, in fact. It was *him*, the shifter guy, the jaguar. How in the hell had he found her?

"I can smell you."

She mentally cursed as his earlier words echoed mockingly within her mind, remembering how acute her sense of smell had been while she had been in her shifted form. He had tracked her. She had never had any chance of escaping him at all.

"I—" Kylie had no idea what to do. She was quite literally backed into a corner, and her options were practically nil. Weak and trembling behind a door, she doubted she could solve her nudity problem by shifting since she both lacked the energy and more importantly, had no idea how to initiate the change in the first place.

Light was pouring through the window beside her, too much for it to still be early morning. Surely she had been passed out for longer than a couple of hours, so where was Paul? Had his plane been delayed?

She needed to stall for time, and that meant getting him talking and playing dumb.

"I—don't have any clothes on," Kylie admitted.

She was completely unprepared for his sudden laugh. "Why didn't you say so in the first place?" he scolded.

Kylie couldn't help feeling slightly offended by his tone. "Maybe it was because I was too busy trying to keep some psycho from breaking into my apartment!" she snapped.

"The door was unlocked," he said pointedly, sounding completely unrepentant.

"And?" she shot back hostilely. "Since when does that

give every asshole on the street permission to waltz into the apartment of someone they don't know?"

"You're certainly taking all of this a lot better than I'd thought you would," he remarked. She could hear the sound of cloth rustling as he talked. "Things may be more serious than I thought."

Suddenly he thrust something dark between the door and the wall. Kylie shrank away instinctually before she saw that it was a thin, navy blue sweater.

"Put that on, and come out. As I said before, for now, I only want to talk."

The sweater was utterly saturated with the smell of him, of something earthy and powerful that she knew she would have never smelled yesterday. The jaguar's senses were muted but very much still a part of her even in her human form.

Her nostrils instinctually flared as she slipped his sweater over her head, his scent starting to make her head spin. She got the feeling that by putting on his sweater, she had just done something that she really shouldn't have done, but between some vague feelings of misgivings and parading out naked in front of some unknown guy, there really was no competition.

Kylie was relieved to discover that the sweater was more than long enough to cover her ass. After pushing the overly-long sleeves up past her wrists, she hesitantly slipped out from behind the door. She half-expected to be met with the sight of a bare-chested man, but the dark-haired man standing only a foot or two away from the door—and completely blocking that potential escape route—was dressed properly in a simple white t-shirt and jeans.

It had been dark back in the forest, and she most definitely had not been herself, so Kylie really didn't remember much about the shifter that had confronted her. Now, she couldn't help but stare as she noted his tanned, well-muscled arms and not just for the obvious reasons. Either he had not been trying too hard to push open the door earlier, or shifting had changed her body even in its human form. She wasn't sure which idea disturbed her more.

Her gaze rose to his face, and Kylie could feel her entire body stiffen as she fought to control her startlement. To say that the guy was hot didn't even begin to accurately describe him. He had the type of chiseled, perfectly proportioned face with plump, luscious lips and just the right amount of stubble on his cheeks and chin to give him that sexy edge that photographers or painters wept over. His eyes, a hazel color more golden than brown regarded her with all the wariness of a predator presented with an unknown entity.

Kylie was grateful for that look. It instantly dragged

her mind out of the gutter it had fast descended into and back to the seriousness of the situation. Her eyes flickered once towards the door to her bedroom. It had a lock, and the window was large enough for her to climb out. Could she make it?

A slight narrowing of her uninvited visitor's eyes was all the answer she needed. The last thing she wanted was to end up tackled on the ground while wearing only an overlarge sweater.

"Okay. Let's talk," she said, gesturing over to the couch.

The smile he flashed her made her heart seize, and now completely irritated with herself, Kylie tore her eyes away from his mouth and stomped over to the couch while the door clicked shut behind her. What was wrong with her anyway? She was beginning to wonder if last night's horrors had robbed her of her sanity after all.

She gave her head a mental shake. Now was not the time to think about her kidnapping. She needed her mind sharp and her emotions stable to safely maneuver the potential minefield this jaguar shifter presented.

Kylie sat on the far end of the couch, making sure his sweater adequately covered all her naughty bits. She watched him approach, all feline grace even as a human.

She was relieved when he sat at the other end of the couch, respecting her personal space.

"So, will you at least tell me your name?" she asked, hating how stiff her words sounded. This was not a man she could afford to show any weakness to, no matter the circumstances.

"Hunter Rivera." He raised an eyebrow expectantly.

She hesitated, but then realized that by knowing her address, finding out her name was only a Google search away.

"Kylie Moore." Then before he could say anything else, she asked, "Do you want to tell me why you think you're entitled to forcing your way into my apartment? Why I should even *talk* to you instead of calling the cops?"

Hunter's eyes suddenly hardened. "Take a good look at your hands," he said quietly. "That's all the permission I need, given it was *you* that entered *my* territory and did what you did."

Wondering if he was trying to trick her in some way, Kylie was reluctant to take her eyes off him, so she raised her hands to eye level instead. She immediately gasped in shock when she realized that her hands were splattered with dried blood. Without a word, she abruptly rose and headed towards her bathroom.

She had already turned on the tap in the sink when

Hunter's large form filled the doorway. He stood there silently and watched with no discernable expression as she vigorously soaped and scrubbed her hands raw until even the blood beneath her fingernails had been cleansed. By then, Kylie's entire body was shaking with the effort of trying to keep it together, and her breathing sounded sharp and panicky. But damned if she was going to fall apart in front of this man without knowing his intentions.

"He's alive you know," Hunter said suddenly, making her jump.

Slowly, she turned to look at him. That wary look had entered his eyes again.

"Although you damned near gutted him, he managed to get back to his car and drive to the outskirts of the city before crashing into an auto repair shop."

Kylie turned her head and looked down at her reddened, damp hands. "He was going to hurt me," she whispered.

She could see him nod out of the corner of her eye. "I was hunting nearby," Hunter said. "I heard you screaming."

"He snuck up behind me when I was reaching into my backseat for my backpack," she continued, the words suddenly tumbling from her lips as if of their own accord. "He knocked me out, and I woke up tied up inside his trunk. He took me into the forest. He had scissors. He started to—started to—c-cut—" Kylie wrapped her trembling arms around her waist and squeezed tightly. "Then I—I—"

"Hey, it's okay," Hunter said gently, reaching a hand out to her, but stopping just short of touching her shoulder. "For now, why don't you go change. I'll be waiting for you in the living room."

Without waiting for a response, he turned and left her to try to regain her composure.

CHAPTER 5

When Kylie walked back into the living room more than half an hour later, now dressed in jeans and a simple long-sleeved shirt, Hunter was seated back on the couch staring pensively at the various picture frames of family and friends that hung on the wall next to the TV. Frankly, she was surprised that he had not barged into her bedroom to drag her out.

She didn't know what to make of him. It was clear that he wasn't going to leave until he received whatever answers he had tracked her down for. For that reason alone, she wasn't quite ready to trust in his professions of not hurting her. Just because he hadn't hurt her *yet* didn't mean he wouldn't later if he felt her answers were less than satisfactory.

Once her trembling had more or less stopped, Kylie had shut herself into her room and quickly threw on the first set of clothes that had caught her eye in her closet. She had even put on a pair of her running shoes, seriously contemplating trying to escape through the window. However, her phone was likely still on the floor somewhere near the front door, and she had never memorized Paul's number. Even if she holed up at a friend's place, Hunter would likely literally sniff her out before Paul could find her.

She was screwed either way, so the best thing she could do was cooperate with Hunter until Paul showed up. At the very least, Paul would add an unexpected variable to the mix, and maybe, just maybe she and Paul would be able to talk their way out of this whole nightmare without raising anyone's suspicions.

It was now almost five hours since she had made it inside her apartment and collapsed in front of the door. Either Paul had been unable to catch a flight home on such short notice and was forced to drive, or his flight was delayed. Whichever it was, it probably wouldn't be long before he arrived. She only had to hold it together for a little while longer…feign ignorance…

"What are you thinking?" Hunter suddenly asked, startling Kylie from her thoughts.

She turned her gaze back to him but didn't move

closer to the couch, nervously bunching the sweater she had planned to return to him between her hands.

"This is a nightmare," she replied. "That's what I'm thinking. People don't turn into freaking leopards, no matter how scared they are."

He scowled. "Jaguars, not leopards," he corrected, an edge to his voice that made her think that particular mistake was often made, though in her case, she had made it purposely. She knew damn well there were only four different cat shifter clans in Riverford, and none of them were leopards. "But you're right. *Humans* don't turn into animals, but *shifters* do."

"*Shifters?*" she echoed with feigned confusion.

"As in shape-shifters." He was watching her face very closely. "Or were-jaguars if that helps you understand it better."

"Were-jaguars...you mean, like *werewolves?*" Kylie exclaimed as incredulously as she could manage. "But—but—last night there wasn't—"

Hunter sighed. "You really don't know anything about this, do you? We don't shift at the full moon if that's what you're thinking."

"How can you be so calm about all of this?" she demanded. "I turned into a freaking jaguar! I nearly *killed* someone, no matter that the sick bastard deserved it! How can any of this be *real?*"

He held up his hands. "Fair enough. Come and sit down. I obviously can't take you to see the Elders when you're this confused. We need to figure out a few things first."

Kylie stayed rooted to her spot. "Elders? What do you mean *elders*? I'm not going *anywhere* with you!"

"No, not yet," he agreed, "but Kylie, let me make something clear right now. You are a shifter, and as such, you are expected to obey certain laws. If it had only been me that witnessed your shift last night, then the situation would not be as dire as it is."

Kylie shrank back in true alarm. "What do you mean?"

"You shifted in front of a human not in the know," he explained, "and that is the one law that must never be broken."

"But I didn't know I could even…!" she protested.

He nodded. "And now that I know that, we can fix this, figure out what happened here."

After staring each other down for a long, tense moment, Kylie finally set his crumpled sweater on the arm of the couch before she cautiously seated herself as far away from him as she could.

"You were adopted weren't you?" Hunter asked.

Her eyes widened. "How could you possibly know that?"

"Because that's the only explanation that would make sense here," he said wryly. "If your parents had been shifters, then there's no way you wouldn't have known about your own heritage, not even if you were a Deadend."

Kylie went positively rigid; she simply couldn't help it.

"What's a 'dead end'?" she asked.

Just saying the word left an awful taste in her mouth. She damn well knew what it meant and had hoped that she would never hear it spoken again for as long as she lived. However, she didn't want to raise his suspicions by not asking the obvious question.

Hunter's lips twisted in what looked like disgust. "It's what kids born to shifter parents are called when they lack the ability to shift. It happens very rarely, but until recently, it was seen as something shameful—a weakness in a shifter family's bloodline or for other, equally stupid reasons. These children were almost always sent to live with humans from the moment their inability to shift was discovered."

"I see," Kylie said frostily. "You think my birth parents abandoned me?"

"Maybe," he replied reluctantly, "or they might have been killed. Lord knows we jaguars have our share of enemies. How you came to be raised by humans could have been for any number of reasons. Some parents are reluctant to give up a Deadend child but do not wish them to grow up with this stigma. Thus, adoption is seen as the best option for the kid."

"But I shifted," she pointed out.

"The fact of which muddies the waters completely. How old were you when you were adopted?"

"Just a baby. Why?"

"And you know *nothing* about your birth parents?" Hunter pressed, ignoring her question.

Kylie frowned. "I would think that was pretty obvious by now."

His lips quirked up. "So far all your reactions have been way different than I had expected, so sorry sweetheart, but there is nothing 'obvious' about you at all."

I'm not your 'sweetheart,' Kylie bristled, but she managed to keep her irritation from her expression. Now was not the time to unnecessarily butt heads with him. She needed to concentrate on getting as much information as she could about him, how much power he truly wielded within his clan, as well as stalling for time.

"Keep smirking like that and I won't answer any more of your questions at all," she warned. "In fact, what even gives you the authority to barge into my home demanding answers in the first place? Those elders you mentioned earlier? Are you some kind of underground shifter cop who answers to only them?"

He made a face. "God no, but the Riverford PD *does* have a few shifters on the force. Which brings me back to the reason why you're currently in deep shit. As I mentioned before, the man you shredded lived. He's currently in the ICU of St. Agnes's Hospital babbling about God sending a girl who turned into a 'leopard' in order to punish him for what he had done to a shit-ton of other girls."

"So he *does* have something to do with all those missing women that have been all over the news lately," Kylie interjected softly, not able to stop the cold shudder that rippled through her body.

"Probably," Hunter agreed. "The bastard was practically begging to confess *something* at the very least, and because the pair of detectives sent down to the hospital happened to include a shifter, the Elders of *all* the Riverford shifter clans know that there was a breach of secrecy. The only reason why they aren't here and I am is because everything you did last night happened within *my* territory, and like it or not, it makes you my responsibility above all others.

"You're lucky—not only that your body picked *that* moment to shift for the first time, but that the bastard's system was pumped so full of a cocktail of illegal shit that it's a wonder he could even stand up straight. Everyone that heard him ranting on and on about his victim turning into an animal just assumed it was the ravings of a druggie tripping out after getting attacked by a mountain lion or bear. As I said before, we can fix this—if you'll let me. But you'll have to plead your case before the Elders. There's no getting around that."

"And if I don't?" Kylie said slowly. "If I refuse to see them, to have *anything* to do with your clan or shifters in general?"

Hunter flashed her a sad smile. "I hope for your sake, sweetheart, that you don't force me to show you the answer."

CHAPTER 6

Kylie was over the arm of the couch and halfway to her bedroom before she heard Hunter's surprised curse, immediately followed by the thump of his shoes hitting the floor heavily as he had likely leaped over the back of the couch as well. Screw stalling. She had heard enough. His implied threat was all the answer she needed. There was no way she could trust any of the shifters. She had to get out of there!

Earlier, she had purposely opened her window while she had been alone in her bedroom in case she had to make a run for it. Her window faced the courtyard of the apartment complex, but more importantly, the small building that housed the manager's office was only about fifty yards away. If she could just make it out the window, at the very least, Hunter would not dare shift in such an open place where anyone looking out their window could see him. With a pursuer only on two feet, Kylie had a better chance of making it to that office, and maybe the humans inside, by their presence alone, would protect her.

Why, *why* had she not escaped earlier while she'd had the chance? No amount of information Hunter *might* have provided her should have been worth the risk of having no escape at all!

With speed driven by panic, Kylie made it through her bedroom door, intent on diving through the window, when what felt like a battering ram hit her squarely from behind, sending her crashing to the carpet with a cry of dismay. She opened her mouth to scream for help, but a large hand clamped over her mouth before she could utter a sound.

Still unwilling to give up, Kylie tried to bite him, but Hunter just pressed his hand harder against her mouth and adjusted his body until his full weight stretched out flat across her back pinned her completely to the floor. She tried to buck him off, to thrash her arms and legs, but she wasn't able to move her body more than a millimeter or two off the floor no matter how hard she strained up against him.

"I'm sorry, but I really can't let you leave," Hunter

said into her ear, his tone genuinely apologetic, damn him. "I know you're scared and confused, but please just calm down. Let me help you, Kylie."

Kylie went limp beneath him, angry and feeling utterly defeated. After a tense, silent pause where neither one of them moved, Hunter cautiously removed his hand from her mouth, but he made no move to get off her. He was right not to trust her, she admitted grudgingly to herself, but that acknowledgment did nothing to lessen the bitterness welling up within her.

Things had been going so well these past twelve years after the agony and sadness of *that* night. College was great, and she had a circle of friends that she really cared about, as well as Paul. She had finally started to feel a sense of safety after none of the things she had feared all her life had occurred. Now, because of one sick bastard, that sense of safety had been thoroughly shattered, and Kylie despaired of ever regaining it.

"I don't want anything to do with all this craziness," Kylie finally said into the heavy silence.

Hunter sighed, his breath warm against the back of her neck, making her involuntarily twitch.

"You can't go back to living as just a human," he said gently. "Even now, the scent of your jaguar is getting much stronger. Other shifters will smell it and know you are one of us. It's dangerous for you to be left as you are now, ignorant of everything a shifter life entails, for both you and the shifters of this city. I could see it in your eyes last night, in your scent, when you faced off against me while we were both in jaguar form. The cat was almost completely in control, and that is something you can never let happen again."

"You make it sound as if I'm possessed by some sort of cat spirit, a demon…"

"Don't worry. It's nothing as sinister as that," Hunter assured her. "You see, we shifters have dual souls. Our human souls are naturally stronger, so I guess you can say human is our default state. Only a bit of the animal is allowed to seep through into our consciousness, to rule our instincts, but last night when I looked into your eyes for the first time, I couldn't see anything that was human. It's a wonder that your human soul was able to come back to the forefront at all."

Kylie closed her eyes, remembering her close call with the teenager in the street. She suddenly felt as exhausted as she had last night.

"Are you saying that I won't be able to keep the jaguar from coming out and taking over my mind?"

"I'm saying that without our help, my clan I mean, that very possibility will hover over you every day for the rest of your life."

Hunter rose from her back and climbed to his feet.

Kylie slowly pulled herself up onto her knees and looked up at the hand he held out to her.

Instead of accepting it, she raised her eyes to his face. "Can you promise me—can you promise me that if I go with you to see your elders, your clan won't lock me up somewhere like some kind of prisoner?"

"We haven't had a Returner in our clan for over a hundred years," Hunter said with a smile. "The last thing those old pussies would want is to alienate a new potential clan member." His expression turned wry. "Especially a female one."

Kylie stiffened. "If they think they can make me marry one of you—"

Hunter's sharp laugh cut her off. "The Elders may wish they could dictate all hookups within our clan, but trust me, if they ever tried, every single one of us would just give them the finger. No, what I meant was that the ratio of jaguar males to females in this city is three to one, so any addition of a lovely lady is always welcome."

Her shoulders relaxed slightly, and she slowly reached up to accept his hand up. Still backed into a corner, Kylie really wanted to trust him, but it would take more than a charming smile and a gorgeous face to break through years of always second guessing everyone's motives. She glanced over at the open window, and she abruptly felt Hunter squeeze her hand tightly. A warning.

With a weary sigh, Kylie turned her attention back to Hunter and deliberately pulled her hand from his grip. She was a little surprised that he let her without any real resistance.

"What now?" she asked.

He regarded her thoughtfully. "I need to explain a few more things, and then I'll take you to speak with the Elders," he said.

A sudden, loud knock at the door had Kylie nearly jumping out of her skin and Hunter turning towards the door with what was unmistakably a low growl.

"Are you expecting anyone?" Hunter demanded, his entire body visibly tense.

A relief like no other instantly washed through her being, nearly making her knees give out. "Yeah, my—"

"Morning sweetie! It's me," Paul's soothing baritone called through her front door.

Kylie automatically started to move towards the door. He had used the code word, the one signifying that it was safe to open the door. However, before she could take more than a couple of steps, Hunter grabbed her arm.

"Don't answer that," he whispered warningly. "If it's

your boyfriend, you can just call him later after all of our business is settled."

Kylie shook her head even as she strained against the hand wrapped around her arm. "I don't have a boyfriend. That's my dad, Paul."

CHAPTER 7

Kylie saw Hunter's nostrils flare as he stared hard at the front door.

"As I thought," he murmured. "He's human."

"He's here to pick me up for lunch," she lied. "My car is in the parking lot. He'll think something's up if I don't answer the door."

Hunter flashed her a skeptical look even as his hand tightened around her arm. "He'll just think you left with a friend."

Kylie shook her head. "I would never bail on my dad without calling him first. The only time I didn't was when I was in a car accident. He's somewhat of a worry-wart, so he'll just think the worst." She clutched at Hunter's arm and did her best to make her eyes plead-ing. "Let me answer the door, *please*! If I suddenly become unreachable, he'll freak out and come looking for me. He might see something he's not supposed to, and I don't want him to get hurt because of me!"

When he still looked unconvinced, Kylie added, "The best thing right now is for me to go to lunch with him and pretend that I wasn't nearly tortured and murdered by some sick bastard last night, much less that I turned into a freaking jaguar! You can follow us, and afterward, I'll go with you wherever you want as long as you promise me that you'll leave my dad out of all of this."

"Kylie!" Paul called again, his voice tinged with anxiety. He pounded on the door three more times in rapid succession.

She grabbed his free hand urgently. *"Please..."*

Hunter looked over at the door once more, before he slowly nodded without a word and released her arm.

Kylie closed her eyes briefly in relief. "Thank you," she whispered sincerely.

More pounding sounded, and she hurried over to the door before Paul decided to break it down. She sensed more than heard Hunter retreat into her bedroom.

"Coming Dad!" she called cheerfully, and the pounding abruptly ceased.

She never called Paul "dad."

"What did I tell you?" Paul scolded as soon as she opened the door.

"I know, I know," Kylie said apologetically as she stepped aside to let him in, "but this time I swear I was ready. I must've just dozed off for a minute at my desk waiting for you."

Paul's pale blue eyes surreptitiously swept the whole room as he entered the apartment. Taking advantage of her back being turned to Hunter's potential spying, Kylie gestured towards the bedroom with her eyes.

His eyes narrowed. "You've got to stop pushing yourself so hard, sweetie. Studying is important, but making time for sleep is even more so."

Kylie looped her arm through his and laughed. "But I always make time for lunch. Let's go. I'm starved."

As they headed for the door, Paul abruptly paused and said, "Don't forget your keys."

Her eyes followed his hand as he pointed down to the floor at her keys and cell phone, both still exactly where she had dropped them after collapsing earlier.

"Oh! They must've fallen out of my backpack when I came in last night."

Truthfully, she had forgotten all about them. The last thing she needed was for Hunter to go through all her contacts and old texts.

After leaving the apartment, neither one of them said another word until they were inside his car and out of the parking lot.

"A shifter was there," Kylie said to his unspoken question, "a guy named Hunter Rivera from the local jaguar clan. He's following us right now. That's the only reason why he let us leave. I convinced him that we had a lunch date and that it would be better to go about my day normally."

"He's the one who saw you?" Paul guessed.

"Yeah. After I called you, I barely made it into my apartment before passing out. He literally sniffed me out and barged into my apartment just as I had finally become conscious again."

"I'm so sorry, Kylie," Paul said, sounding stricken. His hands gripped the steering wheel so tightly that his knuckles had turned white. "There was fog this morning, and my plane was delayed for almost three hours."

Kylie reached over and squeezed his upper arm. "You're here now. That's all that matters to me," she said, her voice rough with emotion.

Paul swallowed thickly and flashed her a tiny smile. "I'll drive us towards downtown. The lunch hour traffic should give you enough time to tell me everything. We'll decide what to do from there."

For the next twenty minutes, Kylie recounted the whole terrible episode, the terrifying realization that her abductor likely planned on using the scissors to cut more than her clothes, even confessing about how close she had come to attacking the teenagers she had stumbled upon afterward. By the time she finished, Kylie was shaking so badly that she wrapped her arms around herself in an effort to control the tremors. Listening to Paul's words of comfort also helped soothe her wounded soul.

"Mom and Dad never once told me that holding on to their humanity while in their shifted forms was so hard," Kylie remarked softly.

"For them, I don't think it was," Paul replied carefully. "Although he rarely did so, whenever Alan would shift in front of me, I never felt as though I was in the presence of an animal. I think it was because no matter what he did, I could always see the human in his actions."

She hugged herself more tightly. "I'm scared, Paul. Hunter says that he only wants to help me, but he also says that he came after me because I broke some major shifter law by shifting in front of that psycho."

Paul glanced at her sharply. "What exactly has he told you?"

"He says that I have to go with him to talk to the elders of his clan, but it sounds more like I'm a criminal about to be put on trial!"

Paul sighed. "I hesitate to say you were lucky after everything you went through last night, but you were extremely lucky that piece of scum took you into a jaguar's territory. From what your father told me, the jaguar shifters of this city are good people if a little bit solitary."

"What are you saying? That I should actually *let* Hunter take me to his clan's elders?" Kylie asked incredulously. "What if they ask me to shift, and I can't do it? Or worse, what if I screw up and they find out the truth about me? I have *no idea* how I shifted in the first place! It just—happened. Wouldn't it be better for me to run? I know you don't know where either my dad's or mom's clans are living, but now that I've shifted, shouldn't I try to find them?"

"Kylie—" Paul said, the hesitancy in his voice making her stomach clench in dread. "I didn't tell you this because I didn't want to needlessly worry you, but I've recently discovered that several Sniffers have managed to infiltrate the city."

Kylie sucked in a sharp breath. "How many?" she demanded.

"I don't know," Paul replied grimly. "Karen said that word on the street was that there were at least four confirmed and a dozen more suspected. There's no way that a shifter leaving the city with a human would go unnoticed, and I'd sooner cut off my left leg than let you try to leave alone. At this point, the best course would be to integrate with the jaguars, to let them act as your shield while we both try to gather more information. Up to this point, we've only had access to information coming from Riverford's cougar shifter clan. Adding the jaguar clan as allies would be a major boon. Lord knows we haven't gotten any closer to finding out what happened to your parents over the past few years."

"If the lions have actually managed to sneak their people into Riverford under such a careful watch, then don't you think the jaguars will be doubly suspicious of a 'human' like me suddenly shifting for the first time in adulthood?" Kylie asked. "Hunter insinuated that this is something that doesn't happen very often. They'll start to dig deeper into my past. Even without the suspicion, you know how important bloodlines are to shifters. I'm not so sure we should risk that level of scrutiny."

"Better the jaguars than the lions," Paul said firmly. "You did say that Hunter fellow told you all the various shifter clan elders in the alliance were informed about you and that Hunter was instructed to bring you in. I can't imagine something as serious as a breach of secrecy would be discussed beyond that level of the hierarchy. If you present yourself before the jaguar clan elders willingly, then we can use that to our advantage. They must believe that you're a—forgive me—Deadend. Given the various social stigmas associated with that word, I don't think they'll see anything wrong with you asking them to keep that part of your history a secret. Let them spread a partial truth—that you are a shifter that revealed yourself to a human in order to save your life."

Paul reached over and grasped her hand, giving it tight squeeze. "This could be a good thing, sweetie."

Kylie flashed him a tiny smile. "I imagine Hunter expected lunch to end with a lengthy car chase. He'll be thrilled."

"It's too bad, though," Paul said with a sigh of—regret? "I've always wondered if participating in a car chase was as much fun as the movies made it look."

Kylie couldn't tell if her adoptive father was joking or not.

CHAPTER 8

After eating lunch at a little Italian restaurant downtown, Paul drove Kylie back to her apartment.

"I'll do my best to keep my cell on me at all times," she said as she unbuckled her seatbelt. "If my phone starts tracking somewhere weird on the locator app or you don't hear from me by midnight, then just assume the worst has happened and call the cops."

"No one at work knows that I'm back in town yet," Paul said, "only that I left the conference because of a family emergency. I can stay at home for the next few days just watching that locator app if I need to." He smiled wryly. "Heck, if I have to go out, it's not as though anyone will look askance at me for staring at my phone screen overly long."

Kylie chuckled and reached for the door handle. She paused.

"Are you sure we're doing the right thing?" she asked, looking back at him a little anxiously.

"Sure? Absolutely not," Paul said seriously, "but given how you suddenly shifting after all this time has thrown pretty much everyone who knows for a loop, I do think this is the best course for now. I'll talk to Karen again this evening and see if anything new has come up regarding the Sniffers along the cougar grapevine."

He reached over and squeezed her shoulder affectionately. "Just keep your chin up and your eyes sharp as always. This may indeed turn out to be a good thing for you."

"I hope so," Kylie replied grimly.

"Once things settle down, we'll talk more about the other."

"Other?"

Paul's eyes flashed momentarily with anger. "The bastard that gave you that knot on your head."

Kylie flinched. After initially telling him about her attack and abduction in the vaguest of terms, she had been trying her damnedest not to think about it at all. Although shifters healed three times as fast as regular humans, the large bump on her forehead was still very much visible. She only hoped it would disappear before she went back to class.

Her mouth twisted. If the jaguars even allowed her to go back to class.

"Okay," she agreed, not quite able to hide the reluctance in her voice.

She had hurried out of the car before her composure crumbled, waving her goodbye as Paul pulled away. Then nervously, she glanced around the lot. Although she had been watching all the cars tailing them down the freeways and streets through the side mirror, Kylie hadn't figured out which vehicle was Hunter's. She had also not seen any vehicles pull into the parking lot after them.

He probably just parked down the street, Kylie reasoned as she turned to head towards her apartment.

For all she knew, Hunter could already be waiting for her inside. She frowned as it occurred to her that he might have left her apartment unlocked when he had left to follow Paul and her.

Just as she reached her unit and was about to reach for the doorknob, Kylie suddenly felt a shiver go down her spine. She whirled around, her heart in her throat and her hands already instinctually rising up in defense before she let them fall back to her sides with a scowl.

"Good. It would have been embarrassing if you

hadn't sensed you were being stalked," Hunter said with a smirk, standing only about a foot away from her.

"Not half as embarrassing as you're about to look writhing around on the asphalt and clutching your balls if you don't wipe that smirk off your face *right now*," Kylie growled. "What if you had made me accidentally turn into a jaguar again?"

"That's exactly what I was testing," he said.

She stared back at him incredulously. "Why would you do that while I'm outside? You were the one who made such a stink about being seen in the first place!"

"Which is why I waited until you were beneath the porch roof to approach you," he replied. "Unless someone is directly behind us, anyone standing underneath is hidden from view."

Kylie turned back to the door. "Please don't ever do that again," she said quietly as she dug her keys out of her pocket. "I'm probably going to have nightmares about that psycho attacking me from behind for the rest of my life, and I don't need any more reminders."

Hunter's hand was suddenly on her wrist, pleasantly warm against the iciness of her skin, making her pause before she could insert her key into the lock. "I think it would be best if we go see the Elders right now. They'll have more news regarding the asshole that kidnapped you. Maybe it'll give you some closure."

She turned back to him. "Where exactly will you be taking me?" she asked, letting suspicion creep into her voice.

"To the forest on the other side of the river along the outskirts of the city," he replied.

"So—what—one of the Elders has a house out there, or do you jaguars have some sort of secret lair?"

"A house, no. The Elders stay in a pretty sweet cave deep within the forest," Hunter said seriously.

Kylie stared at him. He *had* to be pulling her leg.

"You must be joking."

"'Fraid not." He looked her up and down. "In fact, it can get pretty chilly, so you might want to go grab a coat."

So he was the teasing type. Maybe. On any other day, she probably would have humored him, but right now she was in no mood for his or anyone else's games. She would call his bluff—if it actually *was* a bluff.

"Forget it," she said stonily as she jammed the key into the lock. "You must be high if you think I'm going to follow a guy I barely know into a cave deep in the forest to meet a bunch of people I have no way of knowing even exist."

She managed to open the door before Hunter grabbed her arm. She had expected him to panic, to plead, or even apologize. That's why she was thrown a bit off-balance when he doubled over laughing.

"I'm sorry, but the look on your face…" he managed to get out between wheezes as Kylie glared daggers at him. "I take it you're not the outdoorsy type?"

"I like the outdoors just fine," Kylie retorted, jerking her arm out of his grip. "I just don't want to end up as the latest missing persons report on the six o'clock news tonight."

"You're right," Hunter said, swallowing his remaining laughter. "That was incredibly insensitive of me wasn't it? My brother—well never mind. I'm sorry that I upset you. I'm not really taking you to a cave, I promise."

Kylie folded her arms across her chest. "Then where?"

"One of the Elders is Donald Gaither."

Kylie started. His was a well-known name in Riverford society, the CEO of a major architectural firm. This was something Karen had never told them!

Hunter's lips quirked up. "We'll be going to his office downtown. The rest of the Elders should already be there waiting for us."

She hadn't exactly expected something like the Batcave, but she also had not expected to be taken to a regular office building either. The thought of going somewhere so public eased some of her tension. It was still the middle of the day, so the building would no doubt be filled with workers—potential witnesses. They couldn't *all* be shifters, could they?

"Come on. My truck is parked across the street. We can talk more on the way over."

"Fine." Kylie shut and relocked the door. "Why didn't you just park in the parking lot? I knew you were following us, so why all the subterfuge?"

Hunter raised an eyebrow. "You don't smell it?"

Kylie laughed humorlessly. "What *don't* I smell now? You'll have to be more specific."

"It's something sweaty and—oh, I suppose you can say aggressive. There really is no comparison to something a human can smell, so it's hard to explain."

As they began walking to the front of the apartment complex, Kylie inhaled deeply. She instantly wrinkled her nose as the plethora of both familiar and unfamiliar scents strengthened to the point of being nauseating.

"I can smell lots of things that could be described as sweaty," she replied.

He shrugged. "Then I suppose that's one of the first things you'll need to learn—how to recognize the different types of shifters by smell alone. While the scent of a jaguar can be rather pleasant, I can't say the same for all the others with the exception of maybe the other feline-types."

Kylie tensed. "Are you saying that you smell other shifters around here?"

"I really hope that you're near the end of your lease," Hunter said, "because there's no way you can get away with living in this apartment complex for longer than another day or two."

Now Kylie was really alarmed. Exactly what types of shifters had she been sharing a roof with?

"I have no idea what types of animals people might be able to shift into," she lied. "Are there dangerous ones living around here?"

Hunter nodded approvingly. "For a jaguar, yes. This area is the territory of Riverford's black bear clan, and let's just say that bears and jaguars don't exactly get along. They aren't nearly as bad as the alligator clan, but that's a tale better told later."

"Alligators..." Kylie said faintly, feigning shock since she figured it was a reaction Hunter might expect.

Hunter's lip curled up in disgust. "A shifter clan with almost no redeeming qualities save one."

When he didn't elaborate, Kylie prodded, "Which is...?"

His expression was suddenly guarded. "I'll tell you some other time."

Kylie fought to hide her frustration. It seemed she

would have to work harder to get him to part with any information that would truly be useful to Paul and her, especially when he answered with the equivalent of the "I'll tell you when you're older" bullshit that parents often fed to their young children when asked uncomfortable questions. Still, it at least told her there was something worth digging into in regards to the local alligator clan.

Once they were in his black F-150 truck and well on their way down the freeway, Kylie ventured a question, "So, just so I have this straight, are jaguars expected to, I don't know, 'check in' with your elders every once in a while?"

"Do they keep us on leashes, you mean?" Hunter replied dryly.

Kylie merely raised an eyebrow and looked back at him expectantly.

"I think you have the wrong idea about what it means to be part of a shifter clan. What you're describing is more along the lines of being a member of a cult when the clans are nothing more than an extended family of sorts, a community. We don't bow down to the Elders as if they're kings or crap like that. They're just overseers to the interests of the clan as a whole."

"If that's true, then why do I feel like I've just been

picked up by a cop and I'm on my way to the station to be interrogated?" she said pointedly.

He grinned sheepishly. "I suppose you're right, but yours is a special case. Bringing a Returner into the fold is a delicate affair all on its own, but add to that a breach of secrecy—well, sorry but we just can't risk leaving you up to your own devices. Imagine for a moment that the humans ever found out about us, the chaos it would likely cause."

Kylie made a face. "I would imagine that we'd find ourselves either hunted or strapped to a dissecting table in some underground government facility. Well, you don't have to worry about me blabbing about any of this to anyone, not even to my father. I'd likely end up in a psych ward—wait—what do you mean 'returner'? You've used that word once before."

"You remember what I said about Deadends, that they were often sent to live with humans? Well, normally their kids are all born as humans. However, once in a blue moon, a human child with at least one shifter ancestor, no matter how far back in their lineage, can be born as a shifter. Those are known as Returners and are very prized within the clans as they bring new genes into the community. Shifters only make up around one percent of the world's population so you can see that any new addition would be cause to throw a party."

"So—I'm not a Deadend?"

He shook his head. "There's really no way of knowing for sure until we find out who your parents were. I've never heard of a Deadend suddenly developing the ability to shift later in life, but I suppose there's a first time for everything. You being a Returner makes more sense. Either way, it would be better for you to be introduced to the rest of the clan as a Returner."

"And after today, will I be able to go back to my life? I'm missing all my lectures today, you know," Kylie said. "Midterms are coming up at the end of next week. I really can't afford to miss another day. I'm just lucky today wasn't a lab day. Those are a real pain in the ass to make up."

"Senior?" Hunter asked, sounding genuinely curious.

"Junior," she corrected.

Kylie hesitated. Maybe if she offered more information about herself first, then he would be more inclined to share more. She still needed to find out how Hunter figured into the jaguar clan's hierarchy.

"I'm a biology/pre-med major," she added.

"Hmm…so that makes you what? Twenty, twenty-one?"

"Twenty. What about you? What does a jaguar shifter do besides barge into apartments uninvited? Are you in college?"

Hunter laughed. "Not the best first impression, I'll give you that. No, I'm not a student. I manage a few apartment buildings and rental homes in my territory if you can believe it."

Kylie blinked in surprise. "That's the last thing I would've guessed."

He shrugged. "My family's always been in real estate."

"So—if I hadn't shifted while in your 'territory,' then would someone else have come after me?"

"You still think I'm some sort of underground cop don't you?" Hunter said in amusement.

Her eyes narrowed. "Laugh all you want, but how would you feel if you woke up today and found out your reality had become the real nightmare?"

His smile instantly disappeared as he turned to glance at her briefly with a completely unreadable expression in his eyes.

"Is the thought of turning into an animal really so horrible to you?" he asked.

"No," she answered without hesitation, "but the thought of accidentally ripping someone's throat out because I might not be able to control that part of me is."

"I don't think that's going to be a problem, to be

honest," he said, his voice returning to its earlier, friendlier tone. "You didn't lose control even a little bit when I startled you outside your apartment. We'll test it some more, of course, once we meet with the Elders."

"Why do I need to shift at all?" Kylie asked, genuinely curious about how he would answer. "Do shifters get sick or something if they don't change at least every once in a while?"

"Time'll answer that question better than I ever could. As I said before, don't think of shifting as being possessed by an animal. Part of you is human, yes, but the jaguar is equally who you are. Your nature is both. Once the shock of all this wears off, you'll likely find yourself longing to run through the forest, to hunt, as a jaguar."

Hunter paused for a long moment, then glanced over at her, his expression thoughtful.

"After your business with the Elders is finished, I can take you on a trial run through my personal patch of forest if you want," he offered a bit hesitantly.

"Don't you have better things to do than to babysit me?" Kylie asked slowly.

"I think hearing about a couple of stopped up toilets and the latest sob story about why so-and-so'll be late with next month's rent can wait until tomorrow," he said with a grin. "Unless it's something you'd rather do alone…"

Kylie really wished he wouldn't smile at her like that. It made her want to trust him too much, and that was something she could ill afford right now. However, she also couldn't afford to offend what could turn out to be a good ally.

She offered him a tiny smile. "I'll think about it."

CHAPTER 9

The moment Kylie stepped inside the architectural firm, a wave of scents came crashing down on her, making her head swim so much that she had to grab onto Hunter's arm for a moment in order to steady herself.

"Hey, what's wrong?" Hunter asked, his brows knitting in concern as he pulled her off to the side.

"Ugh...how can you stand it?" she muttered, closing her eyes for a moment. "It's like walking into a perfume store after a tornado in here. Is it because there are a lot of shifters here? The smells weren't nearly as in-your-face earlier when I was in the restaurant with my dad!"

"Your body must still be adjusting," he soothed. "Everything should balance out within a few days. Until then, when you're around a lot of people, try breathing shallowly."

Kylie nodded. It was a testament to how over-whelmed she felt that she didn't even try to pull her hand away when he took it. It was even a bit steadying.

They took the elevator up to the top floor. The doors opened up to a large reception room that was surpris-ingly empty except for the lone receptionist at her desk in the center of the room. Her expression was openly surprised.

"Mr. Rivera, we weren't expecting you and your guest for at least another couple of hours," she said, glancing at Kylie curiously.

Kylie mentally snorted. *"Guest" my ass!*

"We can leave and come back if the Elders aren't ready for us," Hunter offered.

"No, no," the receptionist said quickly. "If you both will just have a seat, I'll inform them that you're here. It shouldn't be long."

"I should've asked earlier, but how many elders are there in the jaguar clan? Or is it the same amount in all the clans?" Kylie questioned as they sat down.

"Every clan is different," Hunter replied, "and while only the members of each clan truly know how many elders govern them—and sometimes even *they* aren't completely sure of the whos and how manys—the jaguars currently have ten. I hesitate to call him the head honcho, but Donald Gaither is the Elders'—voice, I suppose is a good way of putting it. Step out of line, or if there's anything important to report, then it'll be him you'll likely be talking to."

"He's rumored to be cold and unfriendly."

Hunter smirked. "Tell him that, and you'll make his day. If he were a wolf shifter, then saying his bark was worse than his bite would've been the perfect description of his personality. He's just really aloof, and that's saying something when talking about jaguar shifters. Socialization isn't very high on our list of pastimes. With the exception of our mates and children, it's just our nature to walk alone."

"I love to hang out with my friends. Now that my jaguar half has been—activated, will being around a lot of people start to irritate me?" Kylie asked worriedly.

"I don't know about irritate, but you might start to feel uncomfortable. Surround a cat with potential enemies, and the first thing he'll want to do is find an escape route. Or a door in a shifter's case. That being said, it's just an instinctual feeling and is not so strong that you can't easily ignore it. Like all the new things you've smelled today, it just takes some getting used to."

The receptionist returned, and Hunter instantly rose to his feet, leaving Kylie to scramble after him. "They're in the largest boardroom."

"Good. That means we can sit," Hunter said, smiling at Kylie. "Follow me."

He led her through a set of double doors to the left of the reception desk into a narrow hall lined with what were probably individual offices. They walked to the end, and Hunter knocked soundly on the door once before he opened it without waiting for a response.

Kylie swallowed against the knot of anxiety that had suddenly formed in her throat and reluctantly followed Hunter into the room. Her eyes immediately did a sweep of the room, noting that there were six women and five men seated all along a long table of cherry oak before her eyes fell on the somewhat familiar, graying man that was seated at the far end. She had seen him a few times at some of the fundraisers she had accompanied Paul to over the years.

"You've caused quite the stir, young lady," Donald Gaither said in lieu of a greeting, his dark eyes boring into her as Hunter and she stood behind the empty chair at the other end of the table.

"Not by choice," Kylie replied stiffly, not daring to break eye contact with him.

He nodded. "Given the circumstances, you should be applauded. The police have had some time to look into your attacker. That human was quite the piece of work. However, we'll get to all of that soon enough. I think introductions are in order first."

One by one, all the Elders introduced themselves by name and occupation. One, Kylie was startled to realize once she got a good look at him, was a history professor she'd had at the university as a freshman. The husband and wife duo sitting next to him were elementary school teachers. Another woman was a police detective. The rest represented a variety of careers from mail carrier to business owners like Mr. Gaither.

Rather than some kind of elite club that Kylie had totally expected, the Elders were a surprising group of individuals that truly represented the different types of people within a community well. Kylie felt some of the tension ease from her shoulders.

"You were one of my students, were you not?" Professor Martinez asked after Kylie had introduced herself.

She nodded. "Intro to World History, yes."

"Interesting. You never once gave off the scent of a jaguar or else I would have noticed. We sometimes get a few jaguar shifter students from Mexico, South and

Central America, or Arizona, but not so many that you, as an unfamiliar face, would have been overlooked. I enjoy chatting about the differences and similarities in our clans."

Kylie shifted her feet uncomfortably. He was showing much more interest in her than she would have liked. A history professor could prove to be especially dangerous, more so if he saw her as a puzzle to be solved.

"Indeed. That such a trauma could awaken your dormant jaguar soul from such a near absolute human state," Mr. Gaither said, looking every bit as interested as the professor.

Kylie swallowed thickly. Or was that suspicion? Suddenly it felt way too hot and confining in the room. She briefly wondered if they would chalk it up to being so new to shifting if she followed all the instincts that were screaming for her to get the hell out of there and darted from the room just like Hunter had mentioned earlier.

"Have you shifted again since?" Professor Martinez asked.

"No. Everything's so crazy right now that I haven't even considered it."

"*Can* you do it again?" Gaither asked shrewdly.

"I don't know," she answered, feeling that it was best to be honest here. "I have no idea how it happened in the first place."

"There's nothing to it," Hunter said, speaking for the first time since they had entered the boardroom. "Desire to be the cat is all you need. Just thinking about shifting with genuine intent behind it will usually do it."

"We wish to see you try," Mr. Gaither said. "Hunter, please take Miss Moore into the office next door so that she may remove her clothing and shift in privacy."

"Come on," Hunter said with a contrite smile, ushering her towards the door with a hand lightly pressing against her back.

"What will they do if I can't shift?" Kylie asked once they were back in the hall and Hunter had closed the door.

"I don't think that will happen, but on the off-chance that it does, they'll probably just ask you to come back next week to give it another go. After all, none of us really knows what to expect with a Returner. Now, I'll be just outside the door. When you shift, give it a *whack* with your paw, and I'll know it's okay to open it."

With my paw... Kylie didn't think she would ever get used to hearing things like that.

After making sure the blinds were drawn across the

huge window, Kylie began to undress, feeling utterly exposed. It was as though she was being initiated into one of those strange secret societies. She could only hope that all her discomfort would be worth it in the end.

Once naked, rather than dwell on all her fears of failure, Kylie took to heart all of Hunter's advice, got down on her hands and knees, and thought forcefully, *I want to shift!*

Immediately, her muscles began to quiver, and before she could gasp in surprise, Kylie felt her body stretch and contort familiarly in that huge muscle spasm she had experienced last time. It was over in a matter of a few seconds, and the first thing she noticed was that she could smell Hunter as keenly as though he was standing right next to her. Looking down, she was met with two black-spotted, gold and white paws.

A strange, chuffing sound came from her throat, the feline equivalent of a laugh, she supposed since she was as giddy as a teen on her first date. It was a completely strange experience to feel herself absently lashing her tail behind her. She was also surprised to find herself itching to go for a run, the walls of the office feeling a thousand times stuffier and more confining while in jaguar form.

Kylie instantly put the brakes on those kinds of thoughts. Her human mind was in control now, and she didn't want to risk losing control again by thinking like a jaguar. Besides, Hunter and a room full of elders were waiting for her so any further explorations of her new form would have to wait for another time.

She trotted over to the door and gave it a sound *whack* with a paw. The door immediately opened to reveal a grinning Hunter.

"I told you, you didn't have anything to worry about," he said.

Kylie chuffed in agreement as she followed him back to the boardroom.

"Excellent," Mr. Gaither said as soon as they entered. "I'm happy that there aren't going to be any problems on that front. As long as you can shift back into your human form just as easily, then we can consider the matter resolved. Hunter, regarding that other problem you mentioned the last time we spoke, do you have any spare units in the building you reside in that you can offer her?"

"Yes."

"Good. We'll arrange movers to take care of the transition on Saturday. In the meantime, put her up in your guestroom. Under no circumstance should she return to that apartment for longer than it takes to grab a change of clothes." Gaither's eyes turned back to Kylie. "You can return back to the office to shift back now. When you return, we'll discuss the human who was the cause of all this as well as the laws within our clan."

Had she been in her human form, Kylie would have been hard-pressed not to make a face. Looks as though she wasn't as off the hook as she had thought.

"Sorry," Kylie said as Hunter and she left the office building a little over an hour later, "but right now I'd rather you just take me home. Having to tell them every-thing about that awful night and then having to listen to all of them drone on and on about shifter laws and etiquette the way they did was exhausting."

"Kylie..." Hunter looked down at her pointedly.

She sighed. "I know, I know. The big bad bears might eat me. Just drop me off at my car, and I'll go stay over at my dad's tonight. I'll tell him that there's a problem with the sewage line in my apartment. That way, he won't be so surprised when I move over to your building. I just need some time to myself to process all of this. Then tomorrow you can take me to meet everyone the Elders 'suggested.' My last class ends at five, and I should be home by five-thirty."

"...okay," he relented. "I'll pick you up around seven. And after that, how about we take that run in the forest I suggested earlier?"

Kylie couldn't help smiling. He was so incorrigible.

"Maybe we can do that too."

CHAPTER 10

"I'm not so sure I like the idea of you living so close to the river," Paul said as they headed out the door early the next morning. "The jaguars may claim the eastern half, but that's never stopped the alligators from pushing their boundaries."

"Don't worry," Kylie replied with a grimace. "Hunter's territory is in the easternmost portion, so there's no reason I'd go anywhere near the contested borders unless it were deliberate. Believe me, between all the horror stories my parents and Karen have told me about the alligator clan, you couldn't pay me to go even to the jaguar territories on the fringes of alligator territory."

"I'll talk to Karen at work and ask her to keep her ears open for anything gator related. They aren't part of the Alliance, but no doubt they've at least heard a few rumors about what happened the other night. I hate to say this, but I'm glad Hunter will be looking after you for the time being."

"Honestly, I'm surprised the Elders didn't make him into my bodyguard or something the way they went on and on about the significance of a Returner. The more Hunter tells me about the clan, the more I'm not so sure joining them was such a good idea. One of the Elders is a history professor at my university, and he looked positively gleeful at the prospect of searching for the identity of my parents."

Paul turned to unlock his car, but not before Kylie saw the troubled look in his eyes. "What's done is done. All we can do now is be extra cautious and try not to do anything that would draw the wrong kind of attention. Once all the excitement dies down a bit, then you can decide whether or not you want to stay here or if we should try to go to the British Isles to look for your mother's clan."

"Let's not think about that right now," she said. "I'll call you tonight after Hunter finishes introducing me to some of the local jaguars."

As Kylie drove to the university, she spent the whole way dreading the onslaught of scents she knew awaited her. She only hoped that Hunter would be right, that her newly enhanced sense of smell had leveled out somewhat overnight. Otherwise, she would have to miss another day of classes—which she could *not* afford —because there was no way she would be able to concentrate with her head spinning. She hadn't really noticed a difference with Paul's scent this morning, but...

As she waited at a red light, Kylie resisted the urge to start banging her head on the steering wheel. Sometimes life just *really* pissed her off, and she didn't need to add a headache to the whole horrible mix.

Besides, the ugly knot on her temple had all but disappeared when she had examined herself this morning. The last thing she needed to do was reintroduce *that* nasty little reminder of just how much life could screw you.

The moment Kylie stepped out of her car, the scents of thousands of people assaulted her senses just as she had feared. Determined not to give up, she stood by her car and just breathed slowly and shallowly as she had back at the architectural firm, letting herself get used to the maelstrom of acrid and earthy scents.

After a few minutes, her head stopped spinning and the smells not quite so potent.

Maybe I can do this after all.

Relieved, Kylie headed towards her first class, hoping

to catch her friend, Molly, before class started to borrow yesterday's notes.

"ARE you sure you don't want to come?" Kylie's friend, Tara, persisted as Kylie walked with her, Molly, and Molly's boyfriend, Ty, towards the parking lot after their last class.

"It's not that I don't want to," Kylie said, pinching the bridge of her nose as if in pain. "It's just my head's been killing me since Genetics. I think yesterday's fever is back. I don't want to get any of you sick."

"Yeah, you are looking kinda pale," Molly said, peering back at her critically. "You probably should've stayed home today, too."

Kylie shook her head. "You know I hate making up labs. The prof probably would've made me come in on Sunday this time. By the way, thanks for the notes."

"No problem. Just make sure they stay in your backpack until at least tomorrow. You're probably long overdue for a good snooze."

"Yes, Mom," Kylie teased.

Molly snorted. "Yeah, laugh all you want, but that's probably why you got sick in the first place."

"We might go clubbing tomorrow night," Tara interjected. "Call me if you feel better, and I'll pick you up."

"Sounds like a plan."

Hopefully, Hunter wouldn't have anywhere else she needed to go. Kylie had a feeling that her list of excuses to her friends would dry up pretty quickly otherwise.

If you have to go a lot of places with Hunter, then there's one excuse that would work for everything, her mind supplied helpfully.

The thought startled her. Then she was irritated with herself. There was no denying that Hunter was hot, but getting involved with him would probably be the worst thing she could do right now, especially when she hadn't even decided if she was going to stay or go hunting her mother's clan.

She snorted. As if getting involved with him was even a problem in the first place. He hadn't shown any romantic interest in her at all. Talk about counting your chickens before they hatch.

Once she was back at her apartment, Kylie began to pack up some of her things into the few boxes she had on hand while she waited for Hunter to arrive. The Elders had told her that they would take care of hiring movers to come on Saturday, and although she had nothing in the apartment that was dangerous for others to see, Kylie still didn't feel comfortable allowing total strangers to handle her more personal items.

While she worked, Kylie let her mind wander to all the potential jaguar shifters Hunter would soon introduce. At the very least, it would be interesting to see if any of them were people she actually knew. There were already a handful of people at her university that she was pretty sure were jaguar shifters. Jaguars and humans were the only two scents she was able to identify with any confidence. Hopefully, Karen would be able to come over to Paul's for lunch on Sunday, and she could add cougar to the list. The rest she would have to ask Hunter to help her with.

She was in the process of packing up the contents of her underwear drawer into a suitcase when she caught a whiff of a familiar scent. Her head was already up and scenting the air before she realized what she was doing. A bit unsettled, Kylie headed for the living room just as a loud knock sounded on the front door.

The scent of a jaguar was strong as she fumbled with the lock. She supposed it was a convenient way to know who—or what—was at the door before she bothered to answer it, but it still kind of freaked her out.

"Hi," Hunter said as soon as the door swung open, a smile lighting up his face, and to her horror, Kylie's heart instantly began to race in excitement.

What the hell was wrong with her? She had *never* reacted to a guy like that, no matter how hot he was.

Embarrassed, she smiled at him tightly before waving him inside. "Just let me go grab my purse and keys, and we can go."

"You're just as tense and wary as the first time I stepped through this door," Hunter remarked. "Did something happen? A bear come sniffing already?"

Kylie pocketed her keys and cell phone and snatched her purse from the coffee table. "No, it's nothing like that. My jaguar side is just freaking me out right now."

Hunter raised an eyebrow. "How so?"

She shrugged uncomfortably. "I'm just not used to reacting to things the way a cat would. It makes me nervous because I'm not sure I *should* be acting that way at all, if maybe I'm letting too much of the jaguar come through."

Hunter's eyes softened in understanding. "You're still worried about losing control."

"Constantly," Kylie admitted, though with more meaning than Hunter could ever guess.

"You shifted forms back and forth with no problem with the Elders yesterday," Hunter reminded her.

Kylie smiled sheepishly. "I know. I keep telling myself that over and over, but—I guess it's because all of this shifter business still doesn't feel natural to me."

"With a few more shifts under your belt, it'll literally become your second nature," he assured her. "Now, we'd better head out. I'd like you to meet a good friend of mine who co-owns a local nightclub nearby, and I think, given your problems yesterday with your sense of smell, it would probably be better to see him now before it gets too crowded."

CHAPTER 11

"*Y*our friend owns *Southern Glacier!*" Kylie
exclaimed as Hunter drove around to the
back of the large, illuminated building and
entered the club's VIP parking garage.

She had expected Hunter to take her to one of the
many small clubs along the edges of downtown that she
and her friends often frequented, not *the* hottest club in
Riverford.

"Co-owns," Hunter corrected with a grin.

"My friends and I have always wanted to come here,"
Kylie admitted, "but I always thought there was no way a
bunch of lowly college students like us would stand a
chance of getting in, so we never tried."

"You'd be surprised," Hunter said. "The owners aren't
as fussy about their patrons as you might think. It's all

just the luck of the draw as long as you're willing to wait in line long enough since people are selected randomly. Really, the owners would let everyone in if they had the room so long as you could pay the cover."

"Even alligator and bear shifters?" Kylie asked shrewdly.

Hunter smiled wryly. "You got me there. No, anyone from the alligator clan is most definitely not welcome. They're naturally—forgive the pun—*snappish*. They can't be trusted to not start trouble. Their tempers are always on a hair-trigger. That's one of the many reasons why they are always at odds with most of the other shifter clans."

"And the bears?"

"They can be aggressive when provoked just like their wild counterparts, but for the most part, as long as their boundaries are respected, they won't cause trouble just for the sake of causing trouble like the alligators. You might see a bear or two in the club, but they tend to not like crowds. Maybe a few jaguars will also show while we're here and I can introduce you."

"A lot of people at the university were staring at me today," Kylie said. "I'm not sure how many of them were jaguars, but I imagine they were shocked that someone that had been human a couple of days ago suddenly smelled like a jaguar."

"I don't think the Elders have gotten around to telling everyone in the clan about you. We don't gather very often, so that's what this little tour of introductions I'm taking you on is all about."

Kylie snorted. "Sounds to me like they're just dumping me on you. I mean, how hard can it be to rent a large hall and just call everyone up and say 'come meet the clan's new member'?"

Hunter chuckled. "Normally I would agree with you, but you're a special case. It's very unusual for a shifter to leave their clan for another unless it's for a mating, so new, unattached additions are pretty rare. It's tradition that they introduce themselves to key members of the clan, but since you're new to all of shifter society in general, it's only logical that they ask me, the only jaguar you're somewhat familiar with, to help you with the introductions."

"So one of the owners of this club is a key member of your clan?" she asked. Knowing just who filled the upper echelons of the jaguar clan could prove useful to her and Paul's search.

"Oh, no. Maxim—that's my friend—heard about you from a family member who's an Elder and wanted to meet you."

There was something about the way Hunter grinned at her as he replied that immediately set Kylie on edge, but she couldn't for the life of her figure out why or even if it was *her* who noticed it or the jaguar in her. She was beginning to wonder if she would ever get used to her dual nature, that maybe she had lived as just a human for too long. What was the use of having enhanced instincts if she couldn't interpret any of their meanings?

Hunter stopped his truck in front of a group of young men dressed in black tuxedoes, and two of them immediately broke away to open their doors. The valet had the strong, earthy smell of a shifter, though it had another underlying element that she had never smelled before. Kylie wondered which type of shifter he was. She would have to remember to grill Hunter later about which shifters were friendly with whom and not just for appearances.

Loud music assaulted her senses once they stepped into the club, from a live band she was pleased to note. She wondered how long Hunter planned for them to stay. It was Friday night, after all, and she was missing out on hanging with her friends. Not that she had much to complain about seeing as she was currently walking into *Southern Glacier* with a super hot guy—and she did *not* just think that.

Kylie's entire body seemed to heat up as she glanced at Hunter from the corner of her eye. Hadn't she already decided that she would keep their relationship strictly on friendly terms, that she wouldn't even try to flirt? It wasn't like her to fixate on any guy, no matter how hot, especially when she knew how dangerous letting this guy, in particular, get closer to her could be.

Even though it was fairly early as far as clubbing was concerned, the tables and dance floor were already pretty crowded. Never had Kylie been so glad about the city-wide ban on smoking in public places than now. She could only imagine the havoc adding cigarette smoke to her already reeling senses would have caused.

Hunter led her through the tables towards the huge bar that spanned the entirety of one of the far walls. He caught the eye of one of the many bartenders and spoke something into his ear that Kylie couldn't hear over the music.

"Have a seat," Hunter said, gesturing towards a barstool that someone had just vacated. "I sent that bartender after Maxim. If you want, I'll buy you a drink while we wait."

Kylie raised an eyebrow as she jumped up onto the stool. She beckoned Hunter closer and said into his ear, "I guess you forgot."

He tilted his head curiously. "Forgot?"

"I'm only twenty remember."

For a couple of seconds, he looked confused before

he shot her an incredulous look. "Normally this would be the last place you'd want to bring that little fact to anyone's attention."

Her smile was self-deprecating. "I'm not much of a drinker." Let him make of that what he will, but the last thing she wanted to do was get into the "whys."

He nodded and then flashed her a smile that was much too charming for her peace of mind. "Even so, my offer still stands. Sparkling water? Coke? Italian soda?"

Kylie couldn't help returning his smile. "Thanks, but I'm good." She gestured with her chin over to the stage where the four-man band was just finishing up a rock song she had never heard before. "Being able to listen to live music is enough for me. I'm usually too busy with school, so it's not something I get to do as much as I'd like."

"Sounds exhausting," Hunter said, leaning up against the bar.

"It can be."

"I never had the 'pleasure' of going to college. When my parents died, my brother and I took over several apartment complexes and rental properties. Occasionally, I will even buy and flip a house. I guess you can say real estate is in my family's blood."

"Is your brother older or younger?"

"Older." Hunter's eyes flickered to the side briefly, his posture suddenly tense.

"You sound pretty busy yourself having to manage that much property," Kylie remarked, deciding not to press the subject. No use purposely stepping on a potential minefield—at least not yet. "I'm sorry that the Elders saddled you with me."

His lips curved up. "Because coming to Southern Glacier with a cute girl is so terrible."

"Well, that was certainly quick," a deep voice abruptly said loudly near Kylie's ear, startling her so much that she nearly fell off her stool.

"Don't even," Hunter said warningly at the tall, platinum blond man dressed completely in black in a fashionable suit sans tie who was smiling affably at them both.

A strong scent of something that was definitely not the scent of a jaguar shifter emanated from him, reminding Kylie of the clean smell of snow in the air. It completely caught her off-guard. She had automatically assumed Hunter's friend would be another jaguar, and now she realized how utterly short-sighted that was of her.

"Maxim Clarke," he offered, holding out a hand to her.

His large hand all but swallowed hers as they shook hands. "Kylie Moore. It's nice to meet you."

The moment she released his hand, Kylie felt a surge of warmth flow through her entire body. It took every ounce of control she had to keep from visibly reacting. What in the hell had just happened? Did Maxim do something to her? Exactly what type of shifter was he?

For his part, Maxim gave no indication that he knew she was freaking out inside, regarding her with the same polite interest in his pale blue eyes. Maybe it was just a natural reaction that shifters of certain clans experienced. Did she dare ask which clan he belonged to? Kylie turned and looked at Hunter questionably, hoping he would understand and save her from asking and possibly committing some kind of social *faux pas*.

"He's a tiger," Hunter said. There was a definite tinge of amusement in his voice.

"Siberian, to be exact," Maxim interjected. "The Bengal tiger clan and we have got a rivalry going on, so you don't want to get us confused."

"At this point, I wouldn't know a Bengal tiger shifter from a moose shifter—if there's even such a thing—so it'll probably be better for everyone all around if I just don't say anything," Kylie said wryly.

Maxim laughed. "Well, come to my family's club often enough, and you'll definitely get a nose-full. You'll ty." He slapped Hunter on the back. "I'm sure this guy'll be happy to set you straight. I'm always telling him he needs to get out more, anyway."

"Your whole family runs the club?"

"Just my older brother, sister, and their mates. You'll find that with shifters, pretty much everything is either family or clan-oriented. Well, with the exception of the jaguar loners. They tend to do their own thing."

"And that's why we have more territory in this city than any other clan," Hunter said.

"Too true, but at least you're not greedy about it like those damn gators," Maxim said darkly.

Hunter's entire demeanor was instantly alert. "More trouble?"

The tiger shifter sighed. "Always," he replied, his tone heavy with meaning. He turned his attention back to Kylie. "The alligator clan hates us felines more than any other. As I'm sure your new clan's elders told you, a Returner like you is a big deal in the shifter world, like winning the genetic lottery. It's only a matter of time before the gators catch wind and see an opportunity to strike back where it would hurt most. When that happens, just know that the Siberians will have your back."

Kylie was taken aback. Was this the reason why

Hunter wanted her to meet Maxim? Did she dare hope that she might have found more true allies within the shifters like Karen? It was still too early to judge, but for the first time in a long time, Kylie felt a flutter of hope that maybe, just maybe she and Paul might be able to move their investigation into her parents' disappearance past the utter standstill it had been in for over a year now.

"Saying thanks doesn't seem like it's enough, but thanks," Kylie said.

He waved a hand dismissively. "I know all this must seem confusing as hell, so the least all of us can do is ease you into our world as painlessly as possible. Which reminds me—a gator tried to start a fight outside the club last Friday and lost his beanie in all the excitement. I'll have security bring it to you so you can get a whiff. That's one scent you'll want to know right away."

"I also have something I want your guys to look at," Hunter said.

"Of course. Did you want to do this now or..." Maxim's gaze flickered over to Kylie meaningfully before fixing on Hunter again.

"Kylie, do you want to go to the back with us, or—" Hunter touched her shoulder, and for the second time that night, Kylie nearly fell off her stool as that same strange warmth she had felt after shaking hands with

Maxim shot throughout her body. However, this time it seemed much stronger, hotter and lingering, as though she had just submerged herself in a hot tub.

Hunter immediately sprang forward to steady her. "Kylie?" he asked worriedly.

"S-sorry," she said, shaking her head as if to clear it. "I just felt dizzy all of a sudden. It's probably just my senses going haywire again."

He frowned. "Maybe it was too soon to bring you into such a crowded place."

She smiled at him with forced reassurance. "I'm okay now. I was only dizzy for a second. You two go on ahead and take care of whatever business you have. I'll just sit here and listen to the band."

When Hunter hesitated, Maxim said, "Don't worry. I'll have a couple of my guys keep an eye on her."

"Okay, but you should at least drink something," Hunter insisted. "Just think of how it'd look if you passed out and I had to carry you out."

This time Kylie's smile was real. "You really do want to buy me that drink," she teased. "Fine. I'll have one of those cherry Italian sodas you mentioned earlier."

As Hunter waved over a bartender, Maxim turned to her and said, "You have a pretty strong scent. I can only imagine it's because you're a Returner. I've never met one before you so I can't compare, but it may pique a few shifters' curiosity." He pointed to a couple of large men who looked like real bruisers standing at the other end of the bar. "I'll have those two make sure no one takes that curiosity any further."

"I appreciate it."

"I promise we won't be long," Hunter said with an apologetic smile as he and Maxim headed away from the bar.

Kylie watched the two men with narrowed eyes as they quickly wove through the throng towards the back of the room with the agility associated with the big cats who were, in essence, their alter egos. For some inexplicable reason, she suddenly had a strong desire to chase after them. Just thinking about going after them made her whole body heat up and buzz with—something. Excitement? She wasn't sure.

Now thoroughly freaked out, she tore her eyes away and concentrated on her drink and the live music. It was no doubt her jaguar side reacting to something beyond her human comprehension. Now was definitely not the time to lose control of her senses, surrounded by a sea of potential enemies.

She could only hope Hunter really wouldn't be gone long.

CHAPTER 12

*I*t was only when she noticed a third pair of eyes, this time from one of the tables close to the bar, staring rather openly at her that Kylie's initial concern started to turn to fear.

The first was a guy sitting four stools down from her. One moment he was chatting with a couple of women, and the next, he froze before turning to look directly at her as if he had suddenly caught her scent in the air. Only—she was pretty sure that he and the rest of the people sitting around her were human.

The second was also a human, an older, thirtyish guy who happened to walk by her. He too had frozen mid-step as if someone had called out to him before turning to look at Kylie with something like bewilderment. This guy had slowly moved on, but sometime when her attention had been on the stage and the band, he had returned to the bar and was now seated at the very end not even trying to hide the fact that he was staring at her with a decidedly creepy expression.

Kylie watched all three warily, wondering if she should wave over the two security guys Maxim had pointed out. It had only been about twenty minutes since Hunter and Maxim had left her at the bar, so she was reluctant to cause a scene that may send them running back to her. There was also the chance that she might be seen as weak within the shifter society, and thus people would be more reluctant to share anything of value with her. Then the opportunity entering the jaguar clan presented would be wasted.

Her eyes flickered over to the security men, and she was a bit startled to see them already looking back at her with twin frowns stretching their lips. They were looking at her as though they didn't like something she was doing, but for the life of her, she couldn't fathom what. It wasn't as though she was encouraging all those creepy stares.

Just as Kylie shot them a puzzled look, a group of seven guys passed in front of them, blocking her view and capturing her full attention. At that moment, she was once again submerged in an inexplicable warmth, and as one, every single guy in that group turned to look at her.

Kylie flinched back in reaction, her heart suddenly speeding up in the beginnings of panic. Her eyes darted around them in an effort to alert the security guys that things had suddenly gone bat-shit crazy, and she inadvertently locked gazes with Creepy Guy Number One who was still sitting four stools down.

Before she could even blink, all seven guys converged on the stool guy, attacking him with fists and kicks. Kylie expected him to cry out for help, but instead, he let out a weird, guttural sound that was purely animalistic and returned blow for blow like a man possessed.

More men began to join the fray as Kylie jumped off the stool and turned with the intent of sprinting for the exit. Instead, she was met with a wall of at least eight men advancing on her with a look of hunger in their eyes like a starving vampire. To add to the horrors, as she crouched into a defensive position, a low growl began to rise on its own accord from deep within her throat, and she could already feel the slight spasms in her muscles that signaled her body was on the verge of shifting.

Shit! Shit!

"Kylie!"

The sound of Hunter's voice in that moment of chaos was as stunning as hearing a chorus of angels. Her head snapped towards his voice in enough time to see him lay out a tall blond guy with a brutal punch to the chin who had tried to block his advance.

She wasted no time in rushing to him, reaching out to grab his arms. "Hunter! What the *hell* is going on! I—"

The moment Kylie touched him, her entire body seemed to ignite with flames, and only Hunter's quick reflexes prevented her from crumbling to the ground. Desire, lust like she had never felt before inundated her mind, her senses, and she found herself lunging at Hunter with a very audible growl, intent on devouring that luscious mouth she had only admired from afar.

Yes—yes—he's the one!

"*Fuck!*" Hunter cursed, thrusting her out at arms-length and shaking his head violently as though to clear it after being punched.

"She doesn't know how to control it!" Maxim's voice penetrated the haze of lust that had almost completely taken over Kylie's mind as effectively as a gunshot in a library, causing her next growl to freeze in her throat. "Get her out of here *now*! I'll take care of things here!"

With another harsh curse, Hunter pulled her tightly against him and began to half-drag, half-march her through the surrounding crowd as fast as he could without sending them both to the ground. Enveloped in his warmth and now mouth-watering scent, Kylie's groin began to throb rather insistently with arousal. She groaned and tried to rub herself against him as they walked, but the constant movement of their legs prevented her from gaining any good friction.

The walk to the VIP entrance seemed to take an eternity, but thankfully Hunter's truck was already waiting for them outside at the curb, doors open and engine running, though the valets were conspicuously absent. By then, all Kylie could think about was getting inside, climbing onto Hunter's lap, and screwing him until they both passed out.

She tried to push Hunter through the opened passenger door, but he grabbed her head firmly between his hands and held steady until she was finally able to focus on his eyes.

"Kylie, you *have to calm the fuck down*," Hunter said sternly, his eyes hard and piercing. "You're in heat, sweetheart, and you're sending out enough mating pheromones to attract the whole state of Texas right now!" He paused and gritted his teeth. "It's taking everything I have in me to keep from ripping your clothes off and screwing you blind right here on the sidewalk," he continued roughly. "I have to get you out of here, but there's no way I'll be able to keep from driving us into a ditch when all I can think about is driving my cock into your body! Try to think of the most un-arousing things as possible...!"

Although she was able to hear every word and she suspected that he was purposely being blunt and crude to shock her, Kylie was having a hard time comprehending them when Hunter smelled *so damn good*. However, some of his desperation managed to seep into her awareness, and enough of Kylie's humanity still remained to want to understand that urgency to fight to the forefront of her consciousness. She was suddenly seeing Hunter as the human woman rather than the jaguar, could see the sweat on his brow and how his entire body shook with the effort of keeping himself from throwing her onto the ground and having his wicked way with her right then and there.

Kylie drew in a sharp, shocked breath, and some of the heat that was scorching her body from within began to cool. At that moment, Hunter looked more animal than man even though he was still in his human form.

I did this to him, Kylie realized with rising horror, *to those men.*

The pinched look on Hunter's face eased, and he slowly released her head and stepped back. His eyes were fixed on her warily as though he expected her to attack him at any moment.

Her body still burned painfully with the need to either mount or have Hunter mount her, and only the horror of the situation prevented her mind from giving over to instinct again.

"Hurry!" she said urgently. "I don't know how much longer I can stay myself!"

Hunter nodded and dashed over to the driver's side while she climbed up onto the passenger seat. She concentrated on shutting the door and buckling her seatbelt, using those simple tasks as an anchor to her sanity. The heat within was a million times worse than the worst fever she had ever had. Hell, just shifting her thighs had her groin throbbing almost unbearably with need. She clenched them together with a quiet groan. A few more minutes and Kylie was afraid she wouldn't be able to keep herself from masturbating in front of Hunter for even just a little relief.

"Hurry!" Kylie repeated pleadingly through gritted teeth, her eyes closed against seeing the living temptation beside her. Her hands clutched the seatbelt across her chest so tightly that her hands were beginning to hurt.

The truck's tires screeched horribly as Hunter peeled out from the curb. She heard several cars honking angrily at them, but Kylie was feeling so miserable that she couldn't even drum up the energy to worry about wrecking. She distracted herself by thinking about what she would do once they arrived wherever Hunter was taking her.

First and foremost, she would jump into the shower turned up to the iciest setting possible. She didn't care if she died of hypothermia. Anything would be better than the burning she was currently enduring. If this was what a female jaguar shifter endured every time they went into heat, Kylie didn't know how they managed without going insane.

"Almost there. Hang in there," Hunter abruptly said, his deep voice reverberating directly through her loins, making Kylie clench her thighs together more tightly with a moan of frustrated agony.

She heard Hunter hiss and wondered if she had accidentally bombarded him with a fresh new pheromone wave of doom. Dammit! Why didn't anyone warn her about this? She had no memories of her mother ever going through something like this!

By the time the truck stopped and she heard Hunter open the door, Kylie was practically writhing on the seat. Her eyes flew open, and not waiting for Hunter's instruction, she all but flew out of the truck. They were in a parking garage she had never seen before. The unfamiliarity of it stopped her in her tracks. She had expected Hunter to drive her to her apartment and thought she could just make a dash for her unit.

Kylie wrapped her arms around her trembling body just as Hunter cautiously walked up to her. "Follow me, but whatever you do, don't touch me. I'll make sure you get into the new apartment I've arranged for you, but for God's sake, don't even think about leaving it until your heat ends. I'll try to find a woman from our clan to come sit with you. She'll be able to explain what's going on with you better than I ever could."

"How long does a jaguar's heat last?" Kylie asked as she followed him into the building, making sure to fix her eyes on his feet.

"Twelve days usually," he replied apologetically.

She hissed in sudden anger, making her momentarily forget about the throbbing between her legs. "There's no way in hell I can miss that much college!"

"Until you learn to control your pheromone output, you'll have to."

Kylie's growl of frustration was all jaguar. She was so upset, she didn't realize that they had reached the elevators and Hunter had stopped to push the button. Her entire front rammed into his back, her aching nipples rubbing against the cotton of her shirt as her breasts pressed against him.

A sharp growl was her only warning before Kylie's

body was suddenly whirled around and her back slammed into the elevator doors, a soft, wet mouth swallowing her gasp of shock. Then her mind blanked as relief and pleasure thundered through both her mind and body.

Somewhere in the far corners of her mind, she had a vague perception of clutching tightly at Hunter's shoulders, of Hunter's hands squeezing her ass and the two of them grinding their pelvises against each other in the most delicious friction she had ever experienced while tongues tangled and they both did their best to suck the breath completely from each other's lungs.

Then the support at her back disappeared, and both Kylie and Hunter stumbled backward into the elevator. That abrupt movement seemed to snap Hunter out of his frenzy long enough to force himself away from Kylie.

"Kylie—you have to—we *can't*—" Hunter ground out with tremendous effort as he blindly searched for the right floor button behind him, not daring to take his eyes off a *very* annoyed Kylie.

But then Kylie cupped his cock through his jeans instead of going for his lips and Hunter's lips and hands were once again on her like a beast before she could even blink. The elevator jerked as it started to rise, causing them to fall against the back wall in a tangle of limbs.

Kylie wrapped a leg around his thigh in order to grind more easily against his swollen member, causing Hunter to bite down hard enough on her bottom lip to draw blood. The salty taste seemed to drive them both into a greater frenzy, and suddenly, kissing and rubbing her body against him wasn't nearly enough.

She reached up to grip the flap of his shirt where it opened just below his neck and yanked down hard. The sound of buttons hitting the metal walls of the elevator sounded almost preternaturally loud to her heightened senses.

Hearing the sudden *ping* of the elevator reaching the designated floor was enough for Hunter to snap out of his pheromone-induced lust and tear himself away for a second time before Kylie could even run her hands up the smooth muscles of his chest. This time he didn't even try to talk to her as he rushed out of the elevator before the doors had even slid completely open, probably figuring she would follow him—as if she could do anything else in her current state.

Hunter was fumbling with the lock when Kylie caught up to him, pouncing on him just as he managed to turn the knob. They tumbled through the door, landing

CRISTINA RAYNE

in a heap onto the soft, beige carpet with Kylie on top more or less straddling his waist. Hunter's willpower had apparently run out again as his arms encircled her waist possessively and his lips met hers aggressively. The sound of ripping fabric reached her ears a second before the cool air of the apartment hit her suddenly bare back. Another hard yank and the elastic of her bra snapped.

Hunter then rolled them until he had settled his hips between her legs. He lifted himself off her body only long enough to rip the rest of her shirt and bra off, tossing them somewhere behind her, before he buried his face between her breasts and took a long, deep whiff of her scent. It was an action her jaguar side found extremely arousing.

He reached up a hand to pinch and fondle one of her breasts before moving to take the hardened nipple of the other into his mouth. Kylie moaned and arched up into that warm, wet suction, the fingers of one hand clutching a handful of his thick black locks while the other had slipped beneath the collar of his opened shirt and was in the process of digging her nails deeply into the firm muscles of his back just below his shoulder.

However, her sex continued to throb with need, and Kylie bucked her hips, trying to regain the fantastic friction she had experienced in the elevator earlier. An answering thrust of Hunter's hips had her murmuring

120

in encouragement. God, she had never wanted another man as much as she wanted Hunter. She had to feel him thrusting inside her *now*!

"Hunter—*please*," Kylie begged, thrusting up against his hardness desperately as he continued to roughly suck and lathe attention on her nipples. "Need...inside me now...!"

She could feel Hunter's entire body tense against her, and her body tightened in anticipation. Then the warmth and weight of Hunter's body were just—gone.

Kylie's eyes flew open in enough time to see Hunter scrambling away from her across the carpet on his butt, the expression on his face a strange mixture of lust and guilt.

"I'm s-sorry!" he rasped, climbing onto his feet with the look of a man who was in agony.

He stumbled over to the door, his body trembling and jerking as though he had to fight through an invisible barrier for every step. His hand reached clumsily for the door as he staggered across the threshold.

"I'll send someone to help you, I promise!" he called in a strangled voice as if even that had been agony, before slamming the door shut so hard that the walls shook.

Plunged into sudden darkness, Kylie lay on the floor, half-naked and so sexually frustrated that she felt as though she was about to explode from it. There was now only one real option left to her that didn't include pleasuring herself until she was raw, and she shuddered at the thought of the ice shower waiting for her as she forced herself to her feet—even as she was grateful that Hunter had been strong enough to even give her the option.

Hunter…

Kylie groaned and wondered how they could be anything but awkward the next time they saw each other. Somehow, she didn't think this desperate feeling of wanting him would go away so easily after the twelve days were up.

CHAPTER 13

Kylie sat shaking on the floor of an unfamiliar shower, her eyes squeezed shut as she hugged her knees tightly to her chest. Already, the ice streams cascading down her body were beginning to feel not quite so biting and painful and still the fires of arousal within her core burned just as hotly as before she had drenched herself in this ice shower.

How long had she been forcing this frigid hell on herself? Thirty minutes? An hour? However long, it was definitely long past the time to admit defeat. Groaning in frustration, Kylie released her knees and moved to shut the water off. Just that small action made the burning within her increase.

She collapsed back onto her butt and wrapped her arms around herself, dripping wet and shivering. What the hell was she going to do now? For one desperate moment, she considered trying masturbation again even though doing so earlier had not brought her any relief but only seemed to stoke the flames within her higher. Did she dare chance another attempt? Maybe if she massaged herself longer this time...

A jaguar's heat cycle wasn't exactly something she'd ever studied, and even if she had, there were no guarantees that a jaguar *shifter* would follow the same patterns. Kylie couldn't believe that every jaguar female had to endure this hell every heat cycle. Just this first time was enough to nearly drive her mad. There *had* to be a way to end this other than doing the deed because there was no way she would be able to handle this torturous arousal for another hour, much less for the full twelve days.

Kylie hugged herself more tightly as a very uncomfortable realization suddenly occurred to her. Yes—at this point, she had very few viable choices. She could try masturbating again with the very big, very likely risk of just making things worse. She could call Hunter and beg him to come back and finish what they had started. It was something that should really be a last resort no matter how much her body was screaming for it. Even if they were safe about it, having sex with a guy she had known for only a couple of days would be just plain stupid.

However, if she was completely honest with herself, it was not only the choice she most needed but the choice she most *wanted*. After all, he did say that he would try to find a female jaguar shifter to come help her, but for all she knew, it could take *hours*.

…or she could just get over the embarrassment of the whole situation and call Paul to send over her mother's old bracelet, a choice that could very well be the riskiest of them all.

"To hell with it," she muttered. "I'm screwed no matter what I do."

She climbed unsteadily to her feet and slowly, carefully, wrung out her hair and stepped out of the shower, trying not to allow the inside of her thighs to rub together. Her eyes flickered briefly to the jeans and panties lying crumbled on the small bath rug, and she scowled. There was no way in hell that she would be able to put them back on in her condition, and as far as she knew, the only other items of clothing in the apartment were the blouse Hunter had ripped from her body and her equally ruined bra.

A wave of heat washed through her body as her mind filled with the memory of Hunter's hands and tongue caressing her flesh, making her shudder and curse harshly as she hastily put a halt to that line of thinking. Clothes—yes, she needed to concentrate on solving that conundrum...

Kylie doubted any of her things had been delivered yet, which meant no towels either. She vaguely recalled stumbling past the outline of a couch in the darkness as she searched frantically for the bathroom without bothering to find a light switch until she had located the desired room.

A couch pointed towards this apartment being already furnished, so there was a slim chance Hunter or someone had already prepared the bed for her. She was really starting to feel the chill in the air and needed to get dry. Sheets or even her ruined blouse would be better than nothing.

She paused only long enough to tug her cell phone out of the pocket of her jeans. Then she hurried to the first closed door down the hall from the bathroom. Kylie nearly wept when a fully-made bed, including comforter, was revealed. The room had only a bed, nightstand, and a small three-drawer dresser, as sparsely furnished as a hotel room.

After tossing her phone on the bed, she went to inspect the closet. To her disappointment, there were only a couple of empty plastic hangers hanging along the clothes bar.

Shivering from both the fever within and the wet chill against her skin, Kylie proceeded to draw down the comforter and strip off the plain white top sheet from the bed. She then dried herself off as best she could with one end, blotting at her skin instead of rubbing so as not to aggravate her condition. Once finished, the dry end of the sheet went around her shoulders to keep her wet hair from dripping down her back.

Only then did Kylie sit gingerly on the edge of the bed and reach for her phone again. Paul always worked an evening shift at one of the hospitals on Fridays, so she prayed that he wasn't unavailable at the moment.

"Paul!" she cried the moment the call connected, unable to keep the desperation from her voice.

"Kylie, what's wrong? Did someone hurt you?" Paul demanded.

Kylie drew in a huge breath and blurted, "I went into jaguar heat, Paul! Hunter was introducing me to one of his tiger friends, and it just hit me. It's pretty bad. I caused a brawl in the middle of Southern Glacier because I couldn't control my mating pheromones!"

"Whoa, whoa! Slow down, sweetie!" Paul soothed, but Kylie could still hear the tension in his voice. He was probably thinking the worst and trying not to scare her by freaking out about it. "Where are you now?"

"I'm in the apartment Hunter gave me." She wrapped

her free arm around her waist in a one-armed hug and hunched over the phone as a sudden surge of heat inundated her entire body. "I'm *dying* here, Paul!" she moaned. "I feel like my whole body is about to burn up from within! Hunter says that I'll be in heat for the next twelve days, and there's no way I'll be able to come out of this still sane! I don't have anything of yours here in this apartment, so I need you to bring something you've used recently. A glass, your toothbrush, a fork, *anything*, and—mom's bracelet."

Silence, then he asked in a voice barely above a whisper, "Is Hunter there with you?"

Kylie let out a hysterical laugh. "If he were, then I wouldn't be calling you. It was all he could do to keep from pouncing on me." Like hell she was going to tell him how far it had really gone. "He made sure I got into the apartment safely and ran for the hills. He's trying to find a female jaguar shifter that might be able to help me, but for all I know, it could be hours before that happens, and I really can't stand this torture any longer!"

"Kylie—you do realize that it may not work?" Paul said worriedly.

Remembering her mother, Kylie squeezed her eyes tightly shut in despair. "Yes, but..."

"Okay. I'll need to run home to grab the bracelet from the safe, but from what your father and Karen have told me, it would be a thousand times worse for a human like me to go anywhere near you when you're in such a state. I'd send Karen, but they're short-staffed in the ER tonight..."

Another wave of fire abruptly surged through her body, making her groin throb twice as badly as before, and Kylie gritted her teeth tightly to keep from moaning. She squeezed her knees more tightly together, but that did little to relieve her increasing arousal.

"Then call Molly and have her meet you at the hospital," she instructed roughly through her teeth. "Tell her I have a really bad case of the stomach flu, and you can't get away from the hospital to bring me medicine. My friends thought I looked sick today anyway, and I used that as an excuse to beg off going out with them tonight. I haven't had the chance to give any of them the address to this apartment, so you'll need to let Molly know I've moved. Just feed her the busted sewage line excuse, and send her over."

"Are you sure you want to bring Molly into this, Kylie?" Paul asked. "Being so mentally and physically unstable right now—you could accidentally shift. I don't need to tell you what could happen if the Elders found out that you had unintentionally revealed yourself to another human within only a couple of days. It wouldn't only be the lions we would have to run from."

This time the wave of emotion that washed through her was of dread rather than arousal. "I know. God how I know, but I'm seriously only minutes away from calling Hunter back here and just letting nature take its course because I'm really scared that the jaguar will take over again and just force me to go find what I need anyway."

Kylie shuddered. "Remember what I almost did to that teenager! I'm still myself right now, but I can't honestly say that'll be true if I have to endure even just another couple of hours of this torment! I don't want to involve Molly, but with you and Karen unable to come... If I can't trust my oldest friend, then who else can we?"

CHAPTER 14

*H*er scent was so strong within his nostrils that Hunter half-expected to turn around and see Kylie sneaking up behind him again ready to pounce. He closed his eyes tightly and groaned frustratingly into his hands as he sat on his couch trying unsuccessfully to will away the painful erection straining for freedom against his zipper. Just the thought of her tumbling them both to the ground again had him on the verge of springing to his feet to go finish what they had started, consequences be damned.

Hell, he could still taste her on his tongue, an utterly unique flavor of salt and a sweet, honey-like musk that all jaguar shifter females possessed. Only Kylie's flavor was at least three times as potent as any other jaguar he'd had the pleasure of sampling over the years. His mouth watered at the thought of licking and sucking on that soft, pale skin and those pert, pink nipples again.

Hunter growled and shook his head violently. Damn it! Now was *not* the time to become fixated on a woman, no matter how good she smelled, how tasty, or how well his body had seemed to fit between her legs...

"Fuck!" he hissed and started to yank hard at his hair on both sides of his head, the sharp pain finally clearing the cloud of lust from his head a little.

He seriously needed to get out of the apartment building, to get as far away from the sexy kitty cat only a meager floor below him that had to be some sort of sex goddess sent to torment him if her pheromones were still affecting him when he was this far away from her.

And that was the problem.

At the moment, he didn't trust himself not to run straight back to Kylie's apartment instead of out the building once he set foot outside his door. That was also the very reason why he needed to drag his head out of his cock and his ass to his truck. If her pheromones were affecting him so strongly, there was no telling if it was because his exposure to them had been so long, or if she had already managed to inadvertently flood part of the building with them while he had sat on his couch trying to pull himself together.

While a few shifter males were living in his building,

the majority were humans. One whiff of Kylie's pheromones could potentially cause a repeat of the brawl she had accidentally ignited back at Southern Glacier. Given that she was likely a Returner, Hunter had no idea what to expect from here on out.

He needed to enlist the help of a female jaguar *now*—one that he could utterly trust to be discreet. The last thing Kylie needed was to be thought somehow damaged in these first days of integrating into the clan. He needed someone who could teach Kylie how to—

Hunter jerked his head up. Of course! Who better to teach Kylie control of her own instincts than a *teacher*? Jennifer Graham to be exact.

Unfortunately, he didn't have her number. He would have to pay her a visit. Hopefully, she and her mate were at home and not out on the town or hunting out in the forest. He didn't want to have to track them down. He needed to get Kylie taken care of, and then he really needed to get back to Southern Glacier and resume his discussion with Maxim.

If Maxim's intel turned out to be legit, and there really were Sniffers spotted *within* the city limits...

It was that thought that finally had Hunter on his feet and heading towards the door. He'd be damned before he let his baser instincts keep him from what he needed to do any longer. Kylie wasn't the only one depending on him right now.

An image of his brother flashed in his mind, immensely helping to keep the cloud of lust from screwing with his mind again as he held his breath and dashed towards the door to the stairs rather than the elevator. Kylie's scent no doubt still saturated the interior. He would definitely need to shut it down and stick an "out of order" sign on that potential powder keg once he reached the bottom floor. The last thing he needed was more trouble.

Hunter raced down the stairs, taking only short, shallow breaths even though he didn't *think* he could smell any of her pheromones in the surrounding air. Thankfully, he made it to the ground floor without incident. He hurriedly shut down the elevator and then headed for the parking lot.

However, when he opened the driver's side door to his truck, Hunter was almost brought to his knees as a wave of lust abruptly thundered through his entire being. He automatically raised his head to scent the air, looking for the female who was emitting such a delicious smell—and then promptly cursed and backed away from the vehicle as though it were filled with vipers. He was such an idiot! He had completely forgotten about the pheromones still trapped within!

He would need to air it out for at least an hour. He'd had the smell of her heat in his head for too long. Being surrounded by it once again could very well drive him feral.

He had no choice. He was already risking too much as it was leaving Kylie alone in the building and hoping her blast of pheromones stayed in her apartment while he went to retrieve Jennifer. Adding another hour or so to the mix could quite possibly be disastrous. He needed Jennifer to come to him.

Baring his teeth in frustration, Hunter dug out his cell phone from his pocket and selected Donald Gaither from his contacts. Before the first ring could even finish, the Elder answered.

"I was beginning to think you planned on trying to sweep what happened tonight completely under the rug," he said dryly before Hunter could utter a word.

Hunter stilled. "It's already gotten out?" he asked slowly.

Gaither snorted. "You two caused such a huge ruckus in one of the most public places in the city. I would be shocked if they didn't already know about it in the next town over."

"It's not like she could help it," Hunter retorted. "How was I supposed to know that she would suddenly go into heat? Or for that matter, her? Kylie's only lived as a shifter for a couple of days for God's sake!"

Gaither sighed. "Given that it's taken you almost an hour after the incident to call me, I hope that means you've properly taken care of her?"

An image of Kylie stretched out half-naked beneath him, cobalt eyes wild with yearning, filled his mind, and a fresh, hot wave of desire washed over him. He shuddered and gritted his teeth against the urge to dash back into the building straight to her soft, eager body.

"She's safe," he replied roughly. "I managed to get her into my guest apartment before anything else happened. I was on my way to Jennifer Graham's when I realized it would be impossible to drive, and I hardly think her mate would appreciate me showing up naked on her doorstep, so shifting is also out of the question."

"Wait! You're not with Kylie at the moment?" Gaither scolded.

Hunter growled. "You know damned well why I can't go anywhere near her right now! With the amount of pheromones she's putting out right now, not even a saint would be able to resist her. It's already a damned miracle I was able to resist her long enough to get her into the apartment. She can't control it *at all*. That's why I called you. I need Jennifer's cell number."

"From what I heard, she had half the club patrons

enthralled and fighting over her," Gaither said thoughtfully, his tone making Hunter's back stiffen straighter than a marble column. That tone only meant trouble.

"I know what you're going to say, Gaither, and you can just let that thought leak right out of your ears because it'll be a cold day in hell before I'll mate anybody!"

"No one said anything about mating," the Elder replied calmly, making Hunter growl into the phone again.

Sometimes Hunter just wanted to punch that meddling bastard right between the eyes just to see *him* rattled for once.

"Are you going to give me Jennifer's phone number or what?" he demanded impatiently.

"Of course."

Gaither paused for a moment, likely searching through his contacts, before he rattled off the number.

"And Hunter," the Elder said before Hunter could hang up on him, "if Mrs. Graham cannot help Kylie with her control, call me *immediately*. I don't need to tell you how important she is to the clan, and we, the Elders, will not allow any harm to come to her if it can be avoided."

"Understood," Hunter said shortly.

It was going to be a long night, he just knew it.

ylie was damned near tears by the time she heard a couple of hard knocks on the front door, followed by her friend, Molly's, voice announcing her arrival.

"I'm in the bedroom!" she called hoarsely, curling up even tighter as she lay shivering in a fetal position with both fever and lust beneath the comforter.

At this point, her arousal had become dreadfully painful, and she had already gone so far as to bring up Hunter's number on her phone before forcing herself to shut it off. It was currently lying across the room where she had thrown it in frustration. She prayed that she hadn't broken it.

"God, your dad wasn't kidding when he said you sounded pretty bad when you called him," Molly said with a worried huff as she hurried over to the bed. "Your face is all sweaty and redder than a tomato!"

Kylie lifted her head a bit to focus on her friend. She was relieved to see nothing but plain old worry and a bit of admonishment in Molly's eyes and not the obsessive, hungry gazes she had witnessed in the club.

"You know I would've never called him otherwise," Kylie said with a grimace.

Molly frowned. "He's your *father*, Kylie. I think it's high time you got over this 'I'm a burden' complex you have. If you had gone in to see him earlier, you probably wouldn't be feeling as shitty as you look right now. And *why* is your hair wet? Were you trying to give yourself pneumonia too?"

Kylie made a face. "The nausea hit me so suddenly, I didn't make it to the bathroom in time. Some of it got on my clothes and in my hair."

Molly set down a blue gym bag and a small white paper bag onto the bed before sitting down next to them. "I wondered why your dad wanted me to bring you a change of clothes, too."

Because he's a genius. Kylie hadn't even thought to ask for clothes.

"Wait, you can tell me later," Molly said as Kylie started to explain her complete lack of clothing. "You're shivering so badly that I'm surprised I can't hear your teeth chattering. Let's get you changed and then you can take the medicine your dad sent."

Even in her misery, Kylie couldn't help but chuckle. "You really do sound like my mom right now."

Molly snorted then gasped when she realized that Kylie was naked beneath the comforter. "You should've at least put your underwear back on!" she fussed.

Kylie shut her eyes tightly and struggled not to groan as the thought of her torn bra made her remember Hunter's mouth and hands on her breasts, sending a new wave of heat and arousal to her already aching sex.

"Never mind the clothes for now," Kylie moaned. "I'm about two seconds away from puking again. Can you please go get me a glass of water for the meds?"

The redhead nodded and dashed out of the bedroom. Kylie wasted no time in tearing open the white paper bag and dumping its contents onto the bed. A silver charm bracelet with several oval-shaped charms the size of a dime, a caramel-colored pill bottle, and a small toothbrush tumbled out.

She reached for the toothbrush with a badly trembling hand, praying that it would indeed be her salvation. She squeezed the bristles tightly in her fist, unsure of what to expect.

A few seconds passed with no noticeable effect, and panic began to slowly creep into her mind no matter how much she told herself she was just being impatient. Then from one heartbeat to the next, like blood seeping from a sudden wound, the terrible heat in her body began to rapidly dissipate, and the throbbing between her legs slowly began to ease.

Kylie drew in a deep breath and couldn't help the sob that burst forth from deep within her when she realized that she could no longer smell anything other than a faint ghost of Molly's perfume lingering in the air. It had really worked!

Cautiously, she set down the toothbrush onto the bed and held her breath. When the painful arousal or the strong smell of human did not return after another few seconds, Kylie finally allowed herself to breathe a sigh of relief.

Before Molly could come back, she used a corner of the comforter as an added precaution to shove the charm bracelet and toothbrush beneath her pillow, careful not to touch the bracelet with her bare skin. She then reached for the gym bag and began rummaging through the clothes.

She had just finished putting on a pair of underwear and was in the process of pulling a long, pale-blue over-sized t-shirt over her head when Molly returned with a glass of water. Kylie was surprised that she had actually found a glass.

"You don't have *anything* in your fridge," Molly announced as she handed Kylie the glass.

Kylie went through the motions of taking a couple of the white "nausea pills" that Paul had sent her, recognizing them as just sugar pills as soon as they hit her tongue.

"The smell from the busted sewage line was just awful," she replied as she settled herself back down onto the bed and curled up beneath the comforters with a fake groan. "This apartment building belongs to the son of an old friend of Paul's, so I was lucky just to get in tonight. The movers won't be bringing my stuff until tomorrow. I was here checking the place out when the nausea hit."

Hopefully, Molly hadn't noticed that her car was nowhere to be found in the building's parking lot.

Molly let out a long-suffering sigh. "I really don't see why you insist on making things so hard for yourself. You should've just went back home instead of worrying about finding another apartment."

"I promised myself I wouldn't, so I won't," Kylie said wearily. True enough, but at least here, her past stubbornness and guilt of accepting too much of Paul's kindness were a convenient cover for what was really going on. "Thanks tons for bringing me the meds, but you should probably head out before you catch my germs. Trust me, you *don't* wanna catch this."

Molly rolled her eyes. "Yeah, your dad lectured me about staying too long. Apparently, this bug's been going around for the last few days. He said a few people have even ended up in the ER badly dehydrated from it. More reason for me *not* to leave you alone."

Crap! She needed to get Molly out of the apartment so she could try to use her mother's bracelet before the female jaguar Hunter promised to send arrived. That was a disaster that she absolutely had to prevent. Her future and Paul's safety depended on it.

Plus, she didn't want to have to lie about the shifter's identity. She was feeling guilty enough as it was about all the lies she had already told her friends.

"Sorry, but I don't want you missing class on midterms week on my conscious," Kylie said firmly. "Please, just do this for me. I promise I'll call you or Paul if I think I might need to go to the ER. I don't want to miss finals either, you know."

Molly sighed noisily. "Fine," she agreed reluctantly, "but I swear if I find you here half-dead in the morning, I'll never trust your word again."

"Deal," Kylie agreed readily. "Besides, I'm sure Paul will come check on me once his shift ends at midnight."

"That does make me feel better. See you in the morning."

"But not too early," Kylie warned, waving a hand weakly at her.

With one final worried look, Molly turned and barely managed to walk a couple of steps before a series of loud knocks sounded at the door. The redhead froze and turned towards Kylie.

"Were you expecting someone else?" she asked curiously.

Kylie made a big show of frowning towards the direction of the front door while inside she was beginning to freak out. Shit! She wasn't ready for the shifter yet! She still hadn't…

Her right hand inched beneath her pillow. "No," she lied, "just you."

"Well, you've only just moved in here today," Molly said. "Maybe it's someone looking for the previous tenants."

Before Kylie could reply, a female voice she didn't recognize yelled through the door loudly, "Kylie! My name is Jennifer Graham. Hunter sent me to see if I couldn't help you get sorted out. Can you come let me in, or is the door unlocked?"

Molly raised an eyebrow. "Who the heck is Hunter?" she asked with way too much interest.

Kylie groaned. So much for keeping Molly in the dark about her shifter acquaintances. Could anything else go wrong?

"The person who lent me this apartment," Kylie replied, deciding that the partial truth was best here and not only because she wanted to appease her guilty conscious. Thinking quickly, she added, "I suppose he was just trying to be helpful. Go ahead and let her in on your way out. I should at least thank her for coming face-to-face before sending her on her way."

"Are you sure? You're still looking pretty red in the face. I can just tell her you're too sick to see anyone…"

"They're doing me a huge favor, so I don't want to be rude. I'll survive."

Kylie slowly sat up again, her eyes flicking anxiously from Molly to the door beyond, afraid that Jennifer would come in without invitation, a disaster to avoid at all costs. She had to stall her, even if only for a few minutes.

"Just let her know I'm sick before you send her back," she instructed as calmly as she could.

Kylie only prayed having Molly speak with Jennifer would give her enough time to do what needed to be done.

CHAPTER 16

*A*s Hunter drove back to Southern Glacier after borrowing Jennifer's car, he couldn't help but feel more than a little guilty about leaving Kylie with another—no matter how capable—while she and the situation were still so unstable. However, not only did he need to help his friend with any remaining damage control, for all of their sakes, he also needed to find out whether or not the wolves in Maxim's security believed he was right about the piece of fabric he had found in his section of the forest.

The wolves had taken the fabric to another room to examine it without Hunter and Maxim's scents getting in the way. However, Kylie's explosion of pheromones had reached them before the wolves could return with their verdict.

Hunter scowled as his mind drifted back to what Maxim and he had been discussing right before they'd had to dash back among the club patrons in order to diffuse the brawl Kylie had accidentally incited. Sniffers —they couldn't have breached the city at a worse time.

As Gaither had said, there was no doubt that word of what Kylie had done in the club had already spread among the shifter clans as well as the news that she was a Returner. It would only be a matter of time before both tidbits reached the ears of the lions and they realized both incidents concerned the same person.

Kylie was going to hate it, but there was no way that his clan could let her out of their sight for even a minute now that the Sniffers sent by the lion shifter clan currently trying to invade the region had managed to infiltrate the city. There was no telling how long they had been lurking within the city or what they had been doing, *who* if anyone they had been meeting.

Even if the Elders didn't quite believe his suspicions about the lions' involvement with all the recent disappearances of various shifters in the last couple of years from not only Riverford but also a few nearby towns, the fact remained that the lion clans *were* known to snatch or hunt the Returners of other clans.

The usual large crowd stood waiting outside Southern Glacier's entrance, and Hunter felt some of the tension from his shoulders ebþ at such a familiar sight. Apparently, Maxim had not been forced to completely close the club for the night as he'd feared.

As soon as the young valet opened his door, Hunter scented the air warily, but only the strong scent of the tiger shifter before him and a weaker combination of the club patrons' various scents flooded his nose. Not even a trace of Kylie's pheromones remained.

"Didn't expect to see you back here so soon," the valet said with a smirk as he took the keys from Hunter.

Hunter sighed and flashed the young tiger a half-hearted glare. "Don't go spreading rumors, now. There's been more than enough trouble tonight without that trouble bleeding into tomorrow, too."

The valet nodded sheepishly. "Yeah, the boss already lectured us about wagging our tongues, so don't worry. He hasn't opened the club back up yet, but it's okay to go in now. Mr. Clarke should be back in his office."

"Thanks."

The sharp smells of ozone and vinegar assaulted him the moment he opened the door to enter the club, though neither was enough to make his eyes or nose burn. He quickly made his way through the empty VIP lounge to one of the employee exits leading to the offices in the back.

The door to Maxim's office abruptly swung open

before Hunter could even reach for the knob. He had probably spotted him through the security cameras.

"I wasn't expecting to see you back here tonight," Maxim said, beckoning him into the office.

Hunter grimaced. "You and everyone else, apparently." He sank into one of the thick, comfortable chairs in front of his friend's desk and rubbed his nose irritably. "I see you used the ozone generator."

Maxim perched on the edge of his desk. "I had to. My boys had a hell of a time getting everyone separated and then evacuated even after you dragged your little hellcat out of here. It was like a hundred females had suddenly blasted the place with their mating pheromones. No one could come in at all to start wiping down the place with vinegar without wanting to either rip each other to shreds or run out front to hump the nearest female in the waiting crowd. It was still pretty early, so the sibs and I figured we could salvage tonight by pumping in the ozone for an hour and then running the air through the filters for another. We were finally able to send the staff in for the vinegar wipe down twenty minutes ago."

"I would say send Gaither the bill, but this one is completely on me."

"Don't worry about it," Maxim said with a shrug.

"The gods of mischief were probably just bored today. Sasha thought it was hilarious."

"She would," Hunter grumbled.

If anyone was a hellcat, it was Maxim's little sister. He still couldn't quite believe Sasha had mated so young. She had seemed such a free spirit.

"Dare I even ask what happened after you left?"

"Almost the worst possible thing," Hunter admitted.

"You slept with her," Maxim said with a nod.

The fact that Maxim had accepted him mating a practical stranger as if it weren't a really big deal really irked him. "I said *almost*," Hunter growled.

"Really? Don't tell me you locked her up in your bathroom or something. She'll have your whole building's tenants murdering each other in no time with that type of pheromone output! Although—I have to say you have some pretty impressive control if you managed to walk away from that brutal amount of 'come fuck me' scent screwing with your brain."

Hunter ran a hand through his hair in agitation. "I don't call rolling around with her on the carpet within two seconds of stumbling into my guest apartment, both of us half naked with one of her tits in my mouth, 'impressive control,'" he growled.

Maxim shook his head and smirked. "Well, maybe

not control, but being able to still tear yourself away with such a delicious, eager meal in your hands shows quite the iron will, my friend. But would it have been so terrible if the two of you had ended up mating?"

"Not you too," Hunter groaned, letting his head fall back onto the back of the chair momentarily in dismay before lifting it in order to fix the tiger shifter with a hard gaze. "You know why it would have…"

Maxim smiled at him sadly. "I have my siblings at least. I would wish that you weren't so alone."

"Right now Kylie is as fragile and naïve as a newborn kitten. What kind of asshole would I be to drag someone that's already been traumatized plenty enough into my problems? She's better off with Jennifer Graham."

"Is that who you left her with?"

"Yeah. I figured the best thing I could do for her was get as far away from that building as possible. Hopefully, Jennifer can help her. At least here I can do something useful."

Maxim waved him off. "Don't worry about helping with the cleanup. My staff's probably almost done, anyway."

"I owe you big time."

Maxim reached over and picked something up from his desk. "I think you have that backward," he said softly as he held out his hand.

Hunter's eyes narrowed. It was the piece of fabric that he had left with the wolves earlier.

He reached over and plucked it from Maxim's hand. "So was I right?"

"Only Jake has actually smelled one of the bastards before when they've been in their most natural state. He says that while the scent isn't an exact match, it's close enough that he can't think of what else it could be."

"Fuck. I found it deep within my territory. It just seems—I don't know—sloppy? Do you think they know we're on to them? Are they just toying with us now?"

"Depends on who that scrap of cloth belongs to—or, if deliberate, who left it there for you to find."

Hunter blew out a frustrated breath. "It could be anyone. Hell, it could even be Gaither."

"I'm sure he'd be thrilled if you truly thought so," Maxim said, "but I'd honestly be shocked if he was the one. He just draws too much attention to himself, has his hand in too many pies. There's no way he wouldn't have slipped up by now if it were him. For now, just keep an eye on that patch of forest. If that piece of cloth wasn't deliberately left there, then I sure as hell want to know what the hell they were doing out there. If they've somehow managed to find a way to breach our perimeter…"

"I usually only patrol that portion of my territory

once a day. I'll up it to at least three times that for the next month or so."

"You know," Maxim said hesitantly, "it might be better if someone other than you patrols the other two times, or better yet, get your neighboring jaguars to follow the same routine. It would look less suspicious."

"That might be a little tricky. Most of my clan are still convinced that I'm grasping at straws, seeing shadows, out of grief. Some of them might humor me for a day or two and then it would be back to business as usual. No one's really going to bust their ass without hard proof."

"True, but a couple of days is better than nothing. Although—maybe just adding the occasional companion on your runs might work just as well. You do, after all, have the perfect excuse for it now."

"You're talking about Kylie, aren't you?" Hunter questioned flatly.

"She won't be in heat forever," Maxim said pointedly. "By then everyone in the city will know that she's a Returner. No one will look sideways at you helping her adjust to her newly awakened jaguar nature, especially when it was Donald Gaither, himself, who asked you to help her integrate into the clan."

"I did offer to take her on a run through the forest," he admitted, "but..."

"For now, just think about it. Spread the word about the extra patrols and see how much mileage you can get out of that. After all, a lot can happen in a week and a half. That piece of cloth could become another dead end before you two can speak without wanting to rip each other's clothes off."

"Thank you very much for that mental image," Hunter groused. "You do realize that I still have a shit-ton of Kylie's scent coating my nose? Hell, I can still *taste* her! I'm starting to wonder if it'll *ever* go away."

"Maybe I should have one of my men bring in a bucket of the vinegar solution they're using for cleanup to dunk your head in," Maxim offered with a laugh.

Hunter merely glared and resisted the urge to flip him the bird. It would just make the teasing worse.

"All joking aside, it really might help," Maxim insisted.

"I'll pass," Hunter replied dryly. "At this point, it's not worth the headache I'd be sure to get. I'll just go stay at my old place, and hopefully, my head and nose will be clear in the morning. I should probably get an early start on those extra patrols."

Suddenly all the humor left Maxim's eyes. "Speaking of patrols, I never did get to finish telling you about the probable Sniffers a couple of my young clan brothers saw walking into Riverford Regional around lunchtime today. Both were cougars, early twenties, and utter strangers. I sent over one of my wolves from my security detail to get a whiff of them as usual, and she confirmed that neither scent belonged to any of Riverford's cougars. Lana managed to get a fairly good picture of them as they left the hospital, and I had Sasha show it to some of her cougar friends. Nobody recognized them. Her friends are trying to find out whether or not anyone from the cougar clan is currently hosting visitors."

Hunter stiffened. "Do you think they were scoping out the hospitals, looking for the bastard that attacked Kylie maybe?"

"Either that or they were sent there to speak with the hospital brass, both of which a potential disaster in the making. Right now I have a few wolves and young tigers tailing them. We should know within a few days whether or not our suspicions are confirmed."

"Maybe then the Elders will take our warnings more seriously. I can also ask the bobcat twins to keep an eye out for them. Do you have a copy of that picture I can give to—"

Hunter's cell phone abruptly rang, causing him to break off mid-sentence as he fished it out of his pocket. His heart sank when he saw Jennifer's name on the screen.

"Hunter, I need you to come back to Kylie's apartment," Jennifer said before he could even completely lift the phone to his ear. "Something—well, *interesting* has happened."

CHAPTER 17

The smell of a female jaguar hit Kylie's nostrils just as a thirty-something brunette woman appeared in her bedroom's doorway. She paused on the threshold as if suddenly startled before entering the room completely, shutting the door behind her.

"Hi, I'm Jennifer," she introduced herself again with a friendly smile.

Kylie made a big show of weakly sitting up in bed. "Kylie Moore. Sorry we had to meet like this."

"I'm only sorry that Hunter didn't think to come to me sooner before things got so out of hand. Although..." She paused and stared hard at Kylie for a long, uncomfortable moment before she moved to settle herself down onto the corner of the bed. "You don't look nearly as bad as I thought you would. From the stress in Hunter's voice, I expected to find you writhing on the floor in sexual agony."

Kylie grimaced. "If you had come just ten minutes ago, you would have seen me incoherent and ready to bash my head against the wall in the hope of knocking myself out, the burning and throbbing were so bad. Then my friend showed up, and while she was trying to get me to go to the hospital, the heat just—stopped."

Jennifer's eyes widened. "Are you telling me that you're no longer in heat?"

"I guess," Kylie replied, letting a hint of uncertainty creep into her voice. "Other than feeling a little warm and lightheaded, that terrible arousal is pretty much gone."

"What were you doing right before the heat disappeared?"

"Just curling up on the bed and telling my friend that I wasn't going to go to the ER. No, wait. I took a couple ibuprofens just to appease her. Could that have done it?"

She frowned thoughtfully. "No, I don't think so, though I've never heard of a jaguar's heat stopping after only a few hours."

"Hunter did tell you I was a Returner, right?" Kylie asked. "Maybe that has something to do with it. Maybe my body is still in flux. My sense of smell is still pretty unstable even though it's already been a couple of days since I first shifted."

"Maybe your friend had the right of it, and I should take you to see one of our doctors," Jennifer fretted. "Hunter told me that your pheromone output was off the charts, and I obviously can't tell if you're still putting them out or have actually stopped completely."

"You can't?" Pheromones were definitely something that had never come up in conversation with either her parents or Karen. "I thought it was just me that couldn't smell them or that the heat was driving me so crazy that I couldn't focus on anything else."

"No female can, except maybe a female wolf shifter, though the verdict is still out on that one. A few of them have claimed that they smell *something*, but what they describe is different than what a male says he smells."

"I may not be in heat anymore, but can you still teach me how to control my pheromones before it hits again?" She shuddered. "I don't want what happened at the club to ever happen again. Imagine if it had happened in the middle of one of my lectures. I would have never been able to show my face at the university again!"

Jennifer flashed Kylie a sympathetic look. "Of course, but first, I think I should call Hunter and let him know what's going on. I'll need his nose to judge whether or not your heat has truly stopped, or if something else is going on."

Images of Hunter pushing her up against the elevator doors while devouring her mouth and the rough feel of him shredding her blouse flooded into her mind, and Kylie could feel her cheeks heat up. "Is that really a good idea? The effect I had on him—on everybody—was pretty extreme. I really don't want to put him in such an uncomfortable position again. Wouldn't it be better for him to stay away until at least morning?"

"Normally I would say yes, but you said so yourself. You're a Returner. For all we know, your irregular heat cycle could be a symptom of something much, much worse. I've heard that Returners can sometimes have severe physiological complications after their first shift. I really do think you need to see a doctor, but I also can't take you out of this apartment without knowing whether or not you're still churning out your mating pheromones."

Kylie resisted the urge to look at her pillow where her mother's bracelet and Paul's toothbrush were still hidden. With two people hovering over her with worry over some imagined problem with her body, there was no way they would allow her out of their sight to properly secure them.

"Even if I've stopped sending out the pheromones, the apartment's probably saturated with them," Kylie reasoned. "Won't that be just as bad?"

"Damn. You're right." Jennifer paused and bit her lower lip, considering. "There's nothing to do but to have you step into the hall when he gets here. If you're no longer sending out mating signals, then we can all move somewhere else to talk. Either way, it'll be a week at least before a male will be able to enter this apartment without falling under your spell."

Her smile took the sting out of those last words.

"If you really think it's best, call him," Kylie said reluctantly.

More than her fear of them discovering the bracelet, she was not at all ready to see Hunter again after the way they had gone at each other like the animals they partially were. Add to that Jennifer, whom she had only met a few minutes ago, and their meeting would probably be doubly awkward.

She comforted herself with the knowledge that at least Hunter wouldn't be coming into the apartment today. Now Kylie just had to make sure Jennifer had left the bedroom before Hunter arrived in order to take care of the bracelet and toothbrush.

"I should probably change," Kylie said, drawing the

comforter from her lap and revealing that she was only dressed in a long t-shirt to the older woman.

Jennifer immediately stood up from the bed. "Of course. I'll just go make my call from the living room."

The second the bedroom door closed, Kylie lifted her pillow off the concealed items and wasted no time in using it to shovel them back into the small paper bag. She then pulled out a set of undergarments, socks, and jeans from the gym bag her father had sent and quickly pulled them on, deciding to just keep wearing the t-shirt.

After stuffing the paper bag into the gym bag, Kylie picked it up and headed out the door. There was no way she would leave it behind if Hunter decided she needed to leave the apartment.

"Your coloring is starting to look better," Jennifer said as Kylie sat down next to her on the sofa.

"That's a relief," Kylie replied. She began to comb her fingers through her still damp, medium-length hair, trying to get the tangles out as best she could without a brush.

"Don't let your guard down just yet," Jennifer warned. "For all we know, you could suddenly go into heat again."

Kylie groaned. "That would totally suck. I have midterms at the end of the week."

She smiled sympathetically. "Then let me see if I can teach you how to control the pheromones while we wait for Hunter to arrive."

CHAPTER 18

*K*ylie froze at the single, hard knock on the front door, her heart suddenly in her throat.

Jennifer reached over and gave Kylie's arm a reassuring squeeze. "Let me speak with him first. I'll call out for you to join us in the hallway when I'm sure he's ready for you."

She swallowed nervously and gave the teacher a curt nod. Kylie told herself she wouldn't watch her leave, unsure she could handle seeing Hunter just yet, but as Jennifer opened the door, she found herself unable to tear her eyes away.

For no longer than a couple of seconds, Kylie's eyes met Hunter's heavy gaze over Jennifer's shoulder before the older woman pushed him back away from the door with a hand to the chest and quickly closed the door behind her. It was only then that Kylie noticed that her chest was burning and realized that she had stopped breathing.

He had met her gaze without an ounce of trepidation —at least outwardly. Did that mean he was already affected by the lingering pheromones that had no doubt blasted him once Jennifer had opened the door, or...

She tore her eyes away from the door and scowled down at the gym bag next to her feet. *Do I even want there to be an "or"?*

Between nearly going insane from her out-of-control heat and dealing with her worried visitors, Kylie hadn't had time to really think about what had happened between Hunter and her. No good would come of denying that she had really enjoyed their brief, frenzied encounter, so she didn't bother wasting energy trying. No surprise there as the guy was sexy as all hell. He was definitely someone she wouldn't mind getting to know better, but...

Why did I have to meet him now *when everything is so messed up?* she lamented with a huge sigh.

Kylie had never been in more danger than she was now that she had joined the shifter community. No matter how lonely she was, hadn't she already decided that getting involved with Hunter was probably not the best idea, especially when she still had no clue exactly what the jaguar clan wanted or expected from her?

But...

She closed her eyes in something like despair. *But nothing. I'll never find out what happened to Mom and Dad if I let myself get distracted here. What I need now is a trustworthy friend within the jaguars, not a lover. I'll just apologize for my behavior and let that be the end of it.*

However, instead of removing some of the weight from her shoulders, her decision only seemed to tighten the knot of apprehension growing in the pit of her stomach. To distract herself, Kylie strained to hear what Hunter and Jennifer were talking about, but it seemed they were purposely speaking in voices that seemed no louder than a whisper to even her enhanced hearing.

It had probably been about ten minutes since Jennifer had stepped outside. Was the older woman only filling him in on her observations, or was he having trouble keeping a clear head? Maybe she should have insisted much harder on waiting to see Hunter until the morning.

Kylie picked up the gym bag and carefully made her way to the door on tiptoe. She was just about to press an ear up against the door when Jennifer suddenly called, "Kylie! You can come out now!"

Her heart instantly sped up, and she paused only

long enough to take a deep, steadying breath before she dropped the bag next to the door and slowly opened it. Hunter was leaning against the far wall, his hazel eyes intent on her as she slowly stepped out into the hall, making sure to quickly close the door behind her before too much of the pheromone-laden air could escape.

Kylie could feel the hairs on the back of her neck stand on end and her body tense as he silently continued to stare at her. She saw his nostrils flare a couple of times as he scented the air, but other than that, he didn't move, didn't blink.

A faint ripple flowed through her muscles, making Kylie stiffen even more. Her jaguar was itching to come to the forefront, but she immediately clamped down on the urge to shift. She could tell that Hunter was testing her, trying to provoke her with such a blatant stare, and damned if she was going to fail.

They stared at each other for a long, seemingly eternal moment before Hunter's lips quirked up slightly and he finally blinked. Kylie found that she could finally breathe freely, her shoulders relaxing as if released from a binding spell.

"Your heat truly has ended—at least for now," Hunter said, though he still made no move to approach her. "There's only a faint whiff of mating pheromones clinging to your body, but it's nowhere near as potent as what you were releasing the last time I was near."

Kylie sighed heavily and closed her eyes briefly in relief. "Thank God."

"I have the number of an excellent doctor within our clan listed in my contacts," Jennifer said. "Now that it's safe for you to leave your apartment, we should get you checked out ASAP."

Her eyes flew open in alarm. "Um—no thank you. The last thing I want right now is to find myself someone's lab rat."

"It wouldn't be anything so drastic," Jennifer insisted, "just a physical and some blood work."

Kylie flashed her a skeptical look even as her mind was beginning to go into full panic mode. There was no way in hell she could allow anyone to draw her blood. That was a disaster that had to be avoided at all costs.

"Somehow I don't think it would stop at a blood sample given that I'm a Returner," Kylie said dryly.

Looking exasperated, Jennifer turned to Hunter. "Tell her it wouldn't be like that at all."

Hunter snorted. "I assume you want her to see Needles. Sorry, but I have to side with Kylie on this one. When has just one blood sample ever been enough for that damned vampire?"

Kylie stiffened. "*Vampire?*"

Jennifer rolled her eyes. "He's just spouting nonsense. Dr. Carter is just very thorough."

"All the same, I think I'll pass this time," Kylie said stubbornly. "If my hormones start going haywire again, I'll consider it."

"But—"

"At any rate," Hunter interrupted, peeling himself off the wall, "it's probably best we take this conversation to somewhere more private. Follow me."

Kylie expected him to lead them down the stairwell, but instead, he began to ascend. Did this apartment complex have a roof terrace? Given that her body was still saturated with residual mating pheromones, it was probably best that they went outdoors where the night air could begin cleansing her of them.

She had noticed Hunter sniffing the air more than once as she and Jennifer had argued. He was still very much being affected by her scent even though he was concealing it very well.

However, after only one flight, Hunter led them out of the stairwell and down the hall to the apartment at the end.

"Another empty apartment?" Kylie asked as he inserted one of the numerous keys from his keychain into the lock. Owning an apartment building was sure convenient.

"No. It's mine," Hunter replied, opening the door.

Given Hunter's wild nature, Kylie was surprised at the tidiness of the living room, looking as unlived-in as the living room she had just left. No empty dishes or half-filled glasses on the coffee table, no scattered mail. Even the TV remote sat neatly in the center of the dark wooden surface. The only evidence that this was truly Hunter's apartment was the faint aroma of Hunter's unique scent that permeated the air.

"You can stay here tonight," Hunter said as he ushered them onto the sofa while he sat on the sofa's arm on the opposite end. "I'll see if I can borrow Maxim's ozone generator and have your new apartment neutralized."

Kylie's heart skipped a beat at the thought of sleeping so near to Hunter. "I think I've already caused you enough trouble tonight. I can just go stay at my dad's until the apartment is sorted out."

Hunter shook his head. "It's probably better for you to stay somewhere where you can be alone for the next few days in case your heat suddenly returns."

"But—what about you?" she asked. "I don't want to kick you out of your own apartment!"

Hunter grinned. "Remember, I own a lot of real estate. I'll be fine."

"I still think Kylie should see Dr. Carter tonight,"

Jennifer spoke up, looking at first, Hunter, then leveling a worried look at Kylie. "This isn't only about the problem with her heat cycle. From what you've told me, her awakening was very traumatic. Her body is likely still transitioning into that of a true shifter. What if her jaguar soul suddenly takes over her consciousness while she's asleep?"

Kylie stilled, and this time her heart started to race for an entirely different reason. Could that really happen again? She hadn't forgotten those initial moments when she had been one hundred percent jaguar, how her thought processes had held no human reasoning. The world had been filled with only enemies and prey. In that state, she could very easily go on a rampage inside of the building.

Her eyes lowered to the hands that lay tightly fisted in her lap. She suddenly had the urge to run to the bathroom in order to scrub them, one that she ruthlessly squashed. No matter her fears, she absolutely could not allow that doctor—or any doctor other than Paul for that matter—examine her again. She had to hold it together, dammit!

"Even so—I've spent my whole life being smothered by a well-meaning doctor if I so much as sneezed," Kylie said as steadily as she could. "Hospitals and doctor offices make me itch."

When Jennifer flashed her a puzzled look, she added, "My father is a doctor."

"Given your ancestry, is there a chance that he might know about shifters?" Jennifer asked with interest.

"No. He's one hundred percent human. So was my mother. I was adopted."

She deflated. "Oh. Sorry."

"It'll be okay, Jennifer," Hunter said. "We can't make her go see Needles if she doesn't want to, but what *I* can do is stay and watch over her tonight."

Jennifer looked at him sharply. "Are you sure that's wise?" she demanded. "I don't mind staying with her tonight."

Hunter shook his head. "If the worst case scenario happens and Kylie inadvertently shifts during the night without her human soul in charge, I think it would be much too dangerous for anyone other than me to be here to confront her. I was there the first time she shifted. Her jaguar knows mine."

It was Kylie's turn to look at him sharply. Yes her jaguar knew his, but even if it had gotten used to Hunter's scent over the last couple of days, what made him think that her jaguar wouldn't decide to attack him again?

His only answer was to stare back at her as if daring her to say something. Unfortunately for Hunter, he didn't know how stubborn she could be when she thought she was inconveniencing others, especially if one of them was someone she was determined not to send the wrong messages to.

Kylie threw up her hands in exasperation. "If you're both so worried about my jaguar soul taking over completely, then the solution's pretty simple. Just lock me inside your guest bedroom for the next few nights until everyone's satisfied I'm in control. I assume it has a lock."

Jennifer shot her an incredulous look before sighing noisily. "The lengths some people will go to in order to avoid going to the doctor truly boggles the mind."

The older woman then turned abruptly and all but stabbed Hunter in the center of his chest with her index finger. "I'll defer to your judgment in this for now, seeing as how Mr. Gaither trusted you to look after her in the first place, but Hunter..." Here her eyes narrowed. "...if you even think for a moment that you might lose control of *your* instincts, you damn well better leave the building right that instant and call me to take over here. I don't care how late it is."

"Of course," he replied easily, seemingly unaffected by her very real consternation.

Jennifer's eyes bored into his for a moment longer before she nodded to herself, satisfied by whatever she had seen in his eyes. "Well, it's getting late; Kylie's had a very trying day, so I'll just see myself out. You two have a good night."

"Thanks for everything," Kylie said sincerely.

Then the teacher was gone, and they were alone with a very big elephant between them.

CHAPTER 19

"You don't have to be so tense around me," Hunter said quietly. "What happened earlier between us was beyond either of our control."

Kylie blew out a frustrated breath. "That's not why I'm—I just—Dammit! I wanted to say I'm sorry, but what I should probably say instead is 'thank you.'"

Hunter tilted his head at her in confusion and Kylie hastened to explain, "I know how hard it was for you to fight such a powerful instinct. As much as that horrible heat was threatening to drive me insane, I imagine that pulling away was also really painful for you. So thank you for giving me a chance to choose how to end my heat on my own terms, even if that meant calling you and begging you to come back in the end. At least then, however this whole mess played out, it would have been *our* call and not those damned mating hormones."

She drew in a deep breath to try to calm her now racing heart. Saying all that had been significantly less mortifying than she had feared, but she was still a little bit embarrassed. Lucky for her that Hunter seemed to have such a calm personality.

"I'm not sure doing what was right warrants a 'thank you,'" Hunter said sardonically, "especially when it's my clan and I that should be apologizing for not warning you about something as important to shifters as the heat."

"And *that* conversation wouldn't have been awkward at all," Kylie said with a small smile.

Hunter chuckled. "Yeah, you're a little too old for the 'birds and the bees' talk. Truthfully, your heat cycle probably wouldn't have even occurred to me until your first one had hit, and even then, I never would have predicted that amount of chaos."

"Because I'm a Returner?"

"Maybe," he replied carefully.

His tone gave her pause. "I know that I was being hardheaded about refusing to see the doctor Jennifer suggested, but I want you to tell it to me straight. Am I being incredibly stupid not to go?"

"I'm probably the last person to give you any kind of medical advice," he said seriously, "and I can understand your fear of being poked and prodded as I hate going to the doctor myself. However, I will say this. What we know about Returners is mainly anecdotal, stories passed on through the generations, so your going into heat without warning, losing control the way you did, could actually be something that happens with all Returners. We would need to find someone with loads more data or talk to a few more Returners personally."

"*Are* there any other living Returners?" Kylie asked.

"I haven't heard of any personally, but that's not really surprising given how rare you are and the natural secrecy within shifter clans. The only reason why other clans know that you are a Returner was that you attacked that bastard in the forest, and he lived to talk. We *couldn't* keep it a secret. It was pretty much the only defense the other clans would have accepted for shifting in front of a human."

"So what you're saying is that even though some of the shifter clans here in Riverford might have a Returner or two living among them, they probably wouldn't admit it if we asked?"

He nodded. "Though I doubt very much another Returner exists in this city right now, I can ask the Elders to contact the Elders of the few other jaguar clans here in the US, but even among our own kind, they wouldn't necessarily admit to having any Returners within their communities. Wouldn't want to risk another jaguar clan wooing them away now would they? Not to mention not wanting any of the lion cla—"

Hunter abruptly cut himself off mid-word, panic flashing briefly in his hazel eyes before his expression reverted back to something more neutral, and he shook his head.

"No, we'd never find another Returner unless they wanted to be found," he concluded as nonchalantly as though it was what he had intended to say all along.

Kylie debated on whether or not to let it slide before deciding that this was probably going to be her best chance to get Hunter talking about the lions without making him question her interest.

"Lions?" she asked, allowing a bit of surprise to color her voice. "There are *lion* shifters?"

"Yes, there're lion shifters," Hunter answered way too casually.

"From your tone, I take it jaguars and lions don't get along," Kylie pressed.

His shoulders stiffened ever so slightly. "There are no lion shifters in Riverford."

"Nice try, but you can't brush off my question so easily. Spill."

"No we don't get along," he replied curtly.

Kylie couldn't help rolling her eyes. "You do realize the less you say, the more I know there is to be said? You've already warned me to stay away from the alligators. Should I be just as worried about lion shifters? Are they all arrogant bastards or something? Do you have a rivalry going like the Siberians and the Bengals?"

Hunter sighed heavily. "You're not going to let this go are you?"

"If the reason why you're so reluctant is because of something personal, you don't have to tell me, but if it's not..." She caught and held his gaze. "After what happened to us tonight, I'd rather not be left in the dark about anything that could become important in the future. I've had enough nasty surprises in the last couple of days to last me several lifetimes."

He ran a hand agitatedly through his hair. "It's because of all those nasty surprises you've had to deal with that I didn't want to bring up the lions just yet, but I suppose I only have myself to blame for slipping up earlier. Just do me a favor first." He rubbed at his nose and grinned sheepishly. "The lion clans are a subject that'll take some time to explain."

"Oh, right. If you would rather wait until morning, then—"

"No, that's not it," he interjected. "It's just you smell

way too delicious right now for my peace of mind. Though only residual, I can still smell some of your mating pheromones mixed in with your usual scent, and I'd rather not test myself anymore tonight."

Once again, his bluntness had heat rising to her cheeks, but she ruthlessly stopped her rising embarrassment before it could take hold, refusing to look away. "Right. I'll just go take another shower. I need to go get the bag with my change of clothes from the other apartment."

"Right now a vinegar spray down will work better," he said as she started to get up. "It'll neutralize the pheromones saturated into your skin and clothes a thousand times better than soap and water. Wait right there, and I'll go pour some in a spray bottle."

Kylie allowed herself to sit back into the couch cushions as she silently watched Hunter head to his kitchen, glad for the open floor plan of his apartment. Despite everything he had done for her, she still didn't trust his motives for his seemingly selfless help. That he had just shrugged off their little tongue wrestling match earlier with an "oh well, what can we do" attitude and didn't seem as bothered about it as she was only added to her misgivings.

She had to find a way to learn his actual standing within the clan and soon. The longer she stayed and interacted with Riverford's shifter society, the harder it would be to leave should she decide she would have better luck seeking out her mother's clan or it suddenly would become necessary to disappear—in more ways than one.

Because despite all her misgivings and embarrassment, she found that she really did enjoy his company.

Soon the acrid smell of vinegar assaulted her newly sensitive nose.

Kylie wrinkled her nose. "I hope you have lots of aspirin because something tells me that I'll have a killer headache before long."

Hunter looked over his shoulder with a concerned frown. "It's already bothering you that much?"

She shook her head. "Not yet, but strong smells have always given me headaches, so I just want to be prepared. This is all still so new to me."

He turned to face her completely. "Maybe it would better if we just waited to talk more in the morning—"

"Are you kidding? I'd never get to sleep, wondering why you're so reluctant to tell me about the lion shifters."

If anything, his frown deepened. "You may not be able to sleep even after I tell you about them," he warned.

How right he was, but his deadly serious tone made

Kylie feel a surge of excitement and hope that he would actually be able to give her some new information rather than the dread she should have felt.

"You make it sound as if they're the shifter version of the boogeyman," Kylie said just as seriously.

"That's a pretty good comparison," Hunter said as he returned to the couch and motioned for her to stand.

"Are you saying they're a clan full of killers?" Kylie demanded.

Hunter began spraying the vinegar lightly down her front, causing her to involuntarily flinch away as the strong smell made both her eyes and nose burn.

"Among other things," he agreed, though he didn't elaborate.

It seemed she was going to have to fish hard for more useful information beyond what was common knowledge among the clans. Given the danger her sudden awakening posed to both Paul and her, Kylie didn't have time to go about this as slowly as she probably should. Time to bring out the big guns.

"And you're *sure* there aren't any lions in Riverford?" she asked anxiously. "It's a big city, after all."

As expected, Hunter's whole demeanor grew noticeably tenser as he lowered the spray bottle. He stared at her for a long moment with an unreadable expression before he sighed and said, "There aren't any lion *clans* in Riverford, but like cockroaches, it's nearly impossible to keep the bastards completely out. They always show up, one way or another."

CHAPTER 20

Kylie sank back down onto the couch, a little stunned that he had actually answered her truthfully given what Paul had told her yesterday about the Sniffers.

"What 'other things' are we talking about here?" she asked.

Hunter resumed his place on the far end of the couch. "What you have to understand about most of the shifter clans, in general, is that we're a fairly cooperative bunch. We've had to be in order to keep ourselves hidden from the humans for so long. However, the lion clans have always seen things differently. Their clans have always been strong, their numbers at least twice that of all the other clans. Back in the day, when each clan was ruled by a single alpha, their alphas were often powerful lords that controlled entire regions, ruling over even the humans, and because of that, they've always believed that everyone, not just the shifter clans, should answer to them.

"Then the human population exploded, and whole shifter clans began immigrating to the 'new world,' and the lions realized that they didn't have near enough the numbers to lord it over us anymore. Needless to say, they were pretty pissed about that. To this day, they've had only one goal—to regain the power they once held. Not just over shifters, but *everyone*. They want to be kings sitting on a world throne."

Even though what Hunter was telling her was nothing new, it still sent a chill down her spine having what first, her parents then Paul had been telling her all her life confirmed by someone outside their circle.

"What is it they're doing exactly?" Kylie asked.

"They're conquering major cities one by one," Hunter replied quite matter-of-factly, "and right under the humans' noses."

"What do you mean? Because the last I checked, I haven't seen any lion armies marching into cities on the news."

The smile on Hunter's lips didn't quite reach his eyes. "Over the past hundred years, the sneaky bastards have been slowly taking control over every aspect of the cities they've been targeting. Businesses, politics, medicine, you name it and the so-called 'pillars of the community' in a majority of the major cities around the world are almost all lions.

"Of course, in the cities with shifter clans, there was a shit-ton of resistance, and at first, most were successful in keeping the lion clans from usurping their territories. Then gradually, as the lions grew their businesses into several multi-billion dollar corporations in everything from global exports to technology, it became nearly impossible for the other shifter clans to keep them out. Once in, it was only a matter of time before the lions controlled all the shifter clans in the region, too."

"Why didn't the other shifters just leave?" Kylie demanded.

Hunter scowled. "In the beginning, some tried, but when several of the shifters that had made a run for it started to turn up dead—in some instances whole families—no one else dared leave."

"Are you serious?" Kylie exclaimed. "Who do they think they are, the mafia?"

"Actually, that's a very good comparison, too. The alpha lion in charge of each city controls everything from the shadows just like a Don, or a kingpin. They have hitmen, or spies, or special ops—whatever you want to call them—too, though the majority of us have come to call them 'Sniffers.'"

"That's kind of unbelievable." Kylie narrowed her eyes at him. "Should I be worried?"

He sighed. "Every shifter who hasn't been forced to bare their throats to those bastards should at the very least be wary. The lions haven't managed to take over any shifter-occupied cities here in the south, but it's not for the lack of trying."

"I meant since I'm a Returner," Kylie elaborated.

His expression instantly clouded. "I don't want to scare you…"

"…but?" she prodded with a bit of firmness.

He rubbed the back of his neck in agitation. "There's really not a good way to put this, but—the lions, they *collect* Returners."

Kylie took in his words without blinking. "I thought for sure you were going to say they put out hits on us. Why in the world would they want to 'collect' us? For ransoms? Bargaining?"

"If only it were just that. No Kylie, they want you for the same reason the clans are so protective of their Returners."

For a moment, she gazed back at him in feigned perplexity before abruptly widening her eyes as though in epiphany. "But I'm a *jaguar*!" she protested.

"Damn it, I figured Jennifer would've told you about that when she was explaining the heat," Hunter said. "Though it doesn't happen very much because the Elders tend to discourage it, we can mate and have children with certain other shifters. Unfortunately for all of us, jaguars can produce children with lions."

"This mess just keeps getting better and better," Kylie grumbled.

She then scooted closer to him and put a hand firmly on his arm, making him instantly go rigid. Since he was actually answering all her questions, maybe it was time to ask the questions she really needed the answers to.

"Tell me the truth, Hunter," Kylie continued sternly. "Are there lion shifters in Riverford right now? Is that why you insisted on staying with me tonight even though you were obviously still struggling to be so close to me? Did Mr. Gaither assign you as my bodyguard?"

Hunter's nostrils visibly flared as his eyes fixed on her, his pupils dilating until only a very small sliver of honey-gold showed. Getting this close to a male who likely still had some of her pheromones swimming around in his head despite the vinegar probably wasn't the smartest thing to do, but Kylie stubbornly refused to back down. She needed those answers, dammit!

Then he abruptly sneezed, and when his eyes blinked back open, the heat that had been building within had faded. "Maybe I was a bit overzealous with the spray bottle," he said with a small, sexy smile as he reached up to rub his nose.

This close and she could smell his heady, masculine scent even through the vinegar. A mad urge suddenly popped into her head as she stared at him, and before Kylie could even think to stop herself, she leaned forward and pressed her lips firmly against his.

A sharp gasp was her only warning before his arms roughly wrapped around her back and she was crushed against his chest. A wet tongue licked insistently across her lips until she instinctually parted them—and suddenly her mind was as hazy and full of pleasure as it had been when Hunter had pushed her up against the elevator doors the first time they had kissed.

We shouldn't...we shouldn't... the reasonable part of her mind screamed, but then her back hit the seat cushions and her mind promptly wrenched to a stop as she felt Hunter grind his hardness roughly against her groin with enough force to make her cry out into the kiss.

Sloppy and hard and wet, it was one of the hottest kisses she had ever had, and Kylie found herself nearly devouring those soft, delicious lips with utter abandon. His stubble scratched against her cheek and jaw, adding to the arousal that was now a throbbing, sweet ache between her legs as Hunter continued to thrust and roll his hips erratically against her.

Kylie squeezed her knees tightly against his hips and thrust her pelvis up against the bulge in his jeans, grinding into his irregular rhythm as she dug her fingers deeply into his shoulders. She frowned as she realized that he still had his shirt on, that they both were still fully dressed.

As if reading her mind, Hunter's hands were suddenly pushing up her long t-shirt over her chest, the rough pads of his fingers making her shudder in excitement as they skirted up her belly to cup her breasts over her bra. He gave them a playful squeeze before he pulled away from their kiss with a sigh, his warm breath tickling her swollen lips.

"I want you so bad right now," Hunter said gruffly, making her eyes fly open in surprise. The last thing she had expected him to do was to talk so lucidly.

Lust-darkened eyes met hers, and for a moment, she couldn't breathe.

"I don't know why, but the vinegar isn't working," he said, gritting his teeth and closing his eyes as if in pain. "Even though my nose is burning, your scent is still driving me crazy!"

Kylie swallowed thickly and tried to make her mouth

work. "I was the one who—who attacked *you*," she finally managed. "You smelled good, too."

The muscles beneath her fingers tensed. "I want you," he repeated softly, his eyes still closed tightly. He pressed his forehead against hers. "I think I've wanted you from the first time I saw you step out from behind your door wearing my sweater. I wanted you when I knew damn well I shouldn't. That's why I want you to tell me to go. I won't take advantage of you when you're a slave to the heat, but I don't think I'll be able to keep myself from you tonight, even if I leave this apartment right now, unless you reject me."

Here his lips curved up. "If you decide you want this once you've got a clear head and you've had a few weeks to make sense of this crazy shifter world, then I promise no power on this earth'll be able to drag me away."

Kylie frowned. *Was* she starting to go into heat again? Even now with her entire body thrumming with arousal, she didn't feel even an iota of that same scorching, intolerable heat of before that had almost driven her insane with mindless need. Right now, she was pretty sure she was just plain old horny. Maybe remnants of the heat were still wreaking havoc with her hormones, but when she had looked at Hunter's gorgeous face smiling so sexily at her, she was pretty sure that she had kissed him because she damn well had wanted to, not because she had been a slave to her jaguar instincts.

Starting anything with Hunter was probably the worst idea she had ever had, but...what if it wasn't? What if he turned out to be the only man who could ever truly understand her, truly help her to find out what had happened to her parents? What if she could someday reveal her secret to him? Could she really afford to get sidetracked from her original intentions when it came to Hunter and the jaguar clan? No, more importantly, could she really walk away from something she hadn't even dared hope for until now?

"The Devil tempts but doesn't force." There had been no truer saying than that, especially when the "Devil" in this instance was the jaguar shifter with a body like a god and the smile of an incubus that was currently lying between her legs.

Slowly, Kylie raised her hands to gently cup his cheeks. Startled, Hunter lifted his head, his entire body beginning to shake with what was likely a gallant effort of keeping a sudden surge of lust triggered by her touch at bay. He looked at her warily.

"I kissed you because I wanted to," Kylie said with a wry grin. "My earlier heat had nothing to do with it—well, I really should say nothing *much* to do with it—and I'm definitely not in heat right now. Maybe hot for you, but nothing as insane as I felt when we went at each other in the elevator. If anything, it's *your* fault for distracting me with such a sexy smile, and I do love a guy with stubble."

Something wild and excited flashed deep within his eyes. "Just when I thought I had you all figured out, you totally surprise the hell out of me."

Then instead of bending down to recapture her lips as she expected, Hunter pulled away completely from her body and sprang to his feet. Before worry that he was going to leave her anyway could creep into her mind, Hunter reached down to her shoulders and pulled her up onto her feet as effortlessly as though she was made of air.

"Let's go take a shower," he said, tugging her towards the hallway. "Damned if I'm going to smell that vinegar for a second longer than I have to!"

CHAPTER 21

*K*ylie had only managed to make it a couple of steps into Hunter's spacious bathroom before he whirled around and abruptly yanked her t-shirt over her head, leaving her to blink at him in surprise as he tossed the shirt behind him as if it had personally offended him. He then stepped up to her until only millimeters separated their bodies, and his hands snaked around her back. She had felt the tension of her bra ease before she realized that he had unhooked it.

"H-Hey!" she scolded with a nervous laugh, running her hands up his chest to grip his shoulders tightly as she pressed against his front. "It's not fair that I'm the first one who's half-naked again."

The top of her head barely came up to the height of

his mouth, so Kylie rose on her tiptoes to press a kiss lightly, teasingly, on his slightly parted lips before he could say anything. When she drew her face slightly back, he was looking down at her with intense, narrowed eyes that warned he was probably a breath away from ripping off the rest of her clothes and bending her over the counter between the double sinks.

While that might be fun in its own way, Kylie wanted the first time they slept together to be a lot more intimate. She wanted to be able to feel the hardness and weight of his body pressing into her, to see the arousal and ecstasy on his face as he plunged into her heat for the first time.

Careful not to break eye contact, she took a small step back from Hunter, briefly meeting resistance from the arms still wrapped around her waist before he reluctantly loosened his hold and allowed her another step back. He fisted his hands at his sides as though he didn't trust them not to reach for her again.

However, that was as far as she needed to go.

Kylie reached for the buttons on his already rumpled shirt, and his entire body completely stilled. She stared into his eyes as she slowly began to unbutton his shirt, watching all the various emotions—lust, anticipation, amusement—flash through them even as heat began to rise in her cheeks.

By no means a virgin, she had never been so bold with the one and only guy she'd slept with. Their sexual encounters had been hesitant and awkward at first, and then over the course of the few months of their relationship, their bed-play had fallen into something that was more comfortable, pleasurable, but not even resembling anything close to passionate.

That was when she had known it was time to end it with him. With her parents leaving her with a huge empty place in her heart, she wasn't about to add an empty relationship to the mix if she could help it.

Afterward, she had felt so jaded that she hadn't much bothered with dating. After all, why bother to date anyone when that person might not ever understand her situation, the burden of her secret that had been slowly eating her up inside for the past twelve years?

Here with Hunter, even though all she was doing was slowly opening his shirt, Kylie had never felt so excited, so *alive*. Her body practically thrummed with all the nervous energy coursing through her. It was all she could do to keep her hands from shaking. She didn't want Hunter to think that she was scared.

Hunter remained as still as a beautiful sculpture as she finally drew both flaps of his shirt aside and slipped the shirt off his shoulders to reveal a tanned, nearly hairless muscled chest that would have been the envy of any guy. Kylie let his shirt drop to the floor, and immediately, she reached over to run both her hands over his pecs, thrilling at the silky-hardness beneath her palms and fingertips.

He shuddered and closed his eyes in pleasure. With a mischievous smirk, she took advantage of his momentary blindness to step in closer and latch her mouth onto one of his already hardened nipples. Hunter nearly jumped clean out of his skin, arms as hard and thick as steel cables instantly enveloping her and crushing her against his body once again before she could do more than run her tongue teasingly over the sensitive nub.

A growl that was all jaguar filled the air around her. She could feel its vibrations tickle her lips as she pressed them more firmly to his areola and circled her tongue around his nipple. Though marred somewhat by the smell of vinegar that very much still emanated from her, the smell and taste of him filled her head, reawakening the throbbing between her legs. Yes, her jaguar knew exactly what it wanted.

Kylie let out a small sound of surprise when she felt his hands slip beneath the waistbands of both her jeans and panties and firmly cup the bare skin of her ass, giving both cheeks an aggressive squeeze.

"We need—to get into—the shower," Hunter ground out, pulling her head away from his chest. "I'm about this close to saying 'fuck it' and taking you up against the wall or bent over the tub. I'd much rather take you while you're soaped up and slippery and smelling only of *you*."

Kylie felt a surge of heat in her groin at his words. "As long as I can see your face, you can make love to me anywhere," she promised, her voice low and sultry as she looked up at him almost bashfully from beneath her lashes.

Hunter reached over and finished pulling off her bra, letting it drop before reaching for the button to her jeans just as she did the same to his. Seconds later she was naked and kicking her jeans away, and Hunter's hands had found their way to her breasts as, equally naked, he pressed himself firmly against her back. He tweaked her right nipple with just enough force to make her cry out in a mixture of pain and pleasure while his other hand kneaded the other.

She was practically putty in his hands as he maneuvered them towards the walk-in shower, stopping only to pull the curtain aside in order to turn on the water. Kylie stepped into the hot spray, and barely had enough time to turn around before Hunter was pulling her towards him for another one of those wild, sloppy kisses she enjoyed. His tongue pushed roughly into her mouth, and they spent the next few minutes trying to lick every inch of the inside of each other's mouth as the hot spray washed a bit of the acrid smell of vinegar from her body.

Then Hunter clumsily reached for a bottle of shampoo from a small ledge cut into the shower wall, nearly dropping it in his haste, and pulled away from the kiss. He poured some into his hands before Kylie could reach for it and began to massage it into her hair. It should have felt weird to let someone else wash her hair, but Kylie's mind was buzzing with too much pleasure to think about anything other than how pleasant his fingers felt running over her scalp.

Soon, she could only smell the faint hint of the vinegar that the water had not completely washed from her skin beneath the much stronger sweet scent of the shampoo mingled with the luscious smell of Hunter, himself. She couldn't help leaning into him and drawing in a deep whiff of that heady smell as his soap-covered hands began to slide down her shoulders and back up again in a teasing caress that made her shiver in excitement.

Before either one of them could get lost in the moment again, Kylie stepped back farther into the spray of the shower and tilted her head back in order to rinse her hair. Getting soap in her eyes was *so* not sexy, she thought ruefully.

She could sense Hunter moving around, and then a

few seconds later, he pulled her from the spray and crushed his lips to hers. She could taste the chlorine-tinged tap water in the kiss.

A different type of sweet aroma than the shampoo assaulted her senses as Hunter began to run something slippery and cool over her back and shoulders with aggressive hands, then down over her ass, making her break the kiss with a gasp and hastily rub the water from her eyes.

He took a step back from her with a predatory grin, his hands rubbing along her sides before sliding over her belly and up to her breasts. His hands were once again covered in suds as he very deliberately began to fondle them, his thumbs brushing over her now aching nipples while his hungry eyes seemed to pierce right through her.

Kylie couldn't help but close her eyes and moan as one of his hands dropped down between her legs and began to slowly massage her clit in exaggerated circles with his fingertips. She soon reached over and encircled his thus far neglected cock in a light grip, eager to return the favor. His breath caught, and his whole body noticeably tightened as she slowly began to stroke her fingers along his silky warmth.

Her eyes dropped to watch their hands pleasuring each other, and once again, a mad idea popped into her head. Kylie sank to her knees without warning, her hand still firmly grasping his cock. It was a beast of an organ, long and thicker than she could have ever imagined, and she felt her throbbing sex grow wetter just thinking about that monster plunging into her.

Resisting the urge to stroke herself, Kylie pressed her lips lightly against the head of his member and flicked her tongue across it. A taste that was all Hunter exploded onto her tongue, different than the salty bitterness she had expected, though there was a hint of that as well. A deep moan blended with the hiss of the shower, sending another strong jolt of arousal to her groin. It made her feel wild and powerful, and she knew she had to make him do it again.

She slid as much of his member into her mouth as she comfortably could, and concentrated on licking firmly along the sensitive nerve on the underside as she sucked him, determined to make him see white despite her inexperience. She felt him cradle the back of her head gently with one hand, but he didn't try to press her forward as she had expected. While struggling to keep a steady rhythm with both her mouth and a hand stroking at the base of his cock, she used the other to tentatively fondle his balls. Hunter's legs trembled, and the hand pressing against the back of her head clenched, fisting her hair.

Then suddenly his hands were gripping her shoulders and pushing her back. She released his cock from her mouth with an audible *pop* before looking anxiously up at him. Had she done something wrong?

His eyes were so dilated with lust that she could no longer see any of the hazel, his breaths coming in sharp pants.

"Not yet. Now it's my turn to make you scream," Hunter growled as he lifted her off her knees before she could even blink and hugged her firmly against his chest. "Hold on to me."

Kylie hastily grabbed onto his shoulders as his hands snaked down her back and grabbed her cheeks in order to hoist her up, her legs automatically wrapping around his slick waist. He then turned and propped her back against the smooth stone wall of the shower. He leaned over to lick the dampness over her lips once before taking her mouth fully, trying his damnedest to suck the breath completely from her.

He thrust his hips roughly against her groin, once, twice, she lost count, his member rubbing along her clit and sending sparks of pleasure up her spine. She squeezed her thighs more tightly around him and dug her heels into his lower back, trying to match him thrust for thrust, but that tantalizing friction wasn't nearly enough. She wanted to *feel* him even more. They had teased each other enough.

"Hunter please!" Kylie gasped against his lips, not caring that she was begging.

His hips had stilled for an agonizing few seconds before the hands squeezing her ass lifted her slightly, and the head of his cock pressed insistently against her opening. She had only another second to feel a bit of trepidation at the memory of his girth before he thrust up sharply and her passage was being stretched to its limits.

She groaned at the slight sting and dug her fingers into the muscles of his back as Hunter steadily pressed deeper, opening her impossibly wide. His mouth lowered to her throat to nip along the juncture of her neck and shoulder, making her jaguar soul shiver at the feel of a predator's teeth so near her throat. He was shaking with the effort of going slow, allowing her to adjust to his size, and later she would no doubt be grateful when she needed to walk again. However, right now she just wanted Hunter to fulfill his promise and drive that silky thickness into her until she screamed.

Kylie rolled her hips in encouragement and lowered her head a bit to lick teasingly along the shell of his ear. Hunter growled more loudly against her neck, and suddenly it was all she could do to hold on as he brutally speared her to the hilt and began to thrust into her with swift, powerful strokes that rubbed her in all the right places. She moaned loudly with abandon as bursts of pleasure shot into seemingly every nerve ending in her body.

Another growl reverberated against her skin, and Hunter suddenly locked her collarbone between his jaws with a firm pressure just shy of breaking skin. The action had the disconcerting effect of simultaneously making her head swim and the sweet pressure building within her sex soar to the brink of exploding. She opened her mouth to shout his name, but what emerged was a strange keening that seemed to snap the last remaining thread of Hunter's control.

His fingers dug deeply into the muscles of her ass with bruising force as his cock slammed into her tight heat with a brutal frenzy that finally made her scream in both shock and ecstasy as her body exploded in an orgasm so powerful that it was almost painful. The muscles of her passage clenched down onto the member still thrusting relentlessly into her, making Hunter gasp and bite down harder on the flesh he held between his teeth, likely piercing the skin.

As she trembled and rode the wave of her climax, Hunter drove into her a few more times in quick succession before he gave one final thrust of his hips that shook her to the core and abruptly released her shoulder, throwing his head back as he came with something that was half-roar, half-moan. For a long moment, he held them in that position, cock still somehow hard and buried as deep as was physically possible in her body while the spray of water behind them began to run lukewarm.

Panting as though she had just finished running a marathon, Kylie let her forehead fall onto Hunter's shoulder, feeling drowsy and content to stay just as they were the whole night if that's what her lover wanted. That had gone beyond any kind of fantasy she could have ever hoped for. That she had almost denied herself such a transcendent experience was a travesty narrowly dodged.

Kylie kissed his damp flesh affectionately, causing him to stir and lift his mouth from where it had fallen against her neck. When their eyes met, their mouths naturally came together in a kiss that was nowhere near as wild and consuming as those that had come before but still just as passionate.

She gasped when she abruptly felt him thrust up into her still-tingling passage.

"Again?" she asked breathlessly against Hunter's swollen lips, gazing at him with hooded eyes as he continued to slowly rock his hips against her, rekindling the fire that hadn't quite been banked deep within her core.

He leered. "That was just the appetizer. For the main course, I want to see you spread out on my bed, shaking with pleasure while I slowly taste every inch of your body before making love to you until you or I pass out."

Kylie ghosted her lips teasingly over his. "We'll see."

Hunter's eyes flashed with desire. "I always keep my promises."

CHAPTER 22

"Um—this is probably the absolute worst time to bring this up, but it just now occurred to me and I'm kind of freaking out about it now, but... I'm not on the pill, and we didn't use any condoms," Kylie blurted out into Hunter's chest as they lay intertwined on his bed after their last round of lovemaking.

She expected the body beneath her to stiffen, but instead, he chuckled, leaving her utterly confused and a little irritated. "It's not funny, dammit!" she hissed, looking up at his grinning face with narrowed eyes. "Maybe mating and having kids is just par for the course for jaguar shifters, but *I* was brought up as a human, and I'm in no way, shape, or form ready to be a mom at twenty!"

He bent down and kissed her on the nose. "Sorry. I shouldn't laugh, but the tone of your voice reminded me of a guilt-ridden kid confessing to stealing a cookie from the cookie jar, like you expected me to scold you or something." He squeezed her waist affectionately. "Don't worry. I swear I'm disease free. Plus, a shifter can only get pregnant when she's in heat, and even then, it's a little hard to conceive. We jaguars usually have to bang like bunnies for all twelve days before the woman'll get pregnant."

"But I'm a Returner, so…" Kylie reminded him.

"True," Hunter replied thoughtfully. "We should probably stay far away from each other when you're in heat." He cradled her face in his hands and began to gently caress her cheeks with his thumbs. "Now that I've had you, there's no way in hell I'll be able to resist you, even if you *have* learned how to control your pheromones. It's a damn miracle that I was able to drag myself away earlier, so let's not push our luck."

Kylie felt her tension instantly melt away. "Thank God for small favors."

Hunter released her face, and Kylie laid her head back onto his chest as he wrapped an arm around her waist. He then slowly began to thread his fingers through her hair.

She sighed. It was strange how comfortable she felt cuddling with Hunter like this. Had it only been a couple of hours ago that she had been scoffing at jumping into bed with a guy she had barely known for a couple of days? While by no means a prude, she had never been so uninhibited as she had been today. She had dated her last boyfriend for a couple of months before they had even gone beyond heavy petting to sex, and before him, there had rarely been any intimate touching at all.

Maybe losing control of her first heat wasn't so surprising after all. Kylie absently wondered how Paul was going to react to the change in relationship status of Hunter and her—

"Oh crap!" Kylie suddenly cried, her head shooting up and nearly making Hunter pull a clump of her hair out at the root. "I forgot to call my dad back! He called me right after you left me writhing on the floor from the heat."

Hunter frowned. "That makes me sound like a complete douchebag, doesn't it? I really am sorry you had to go through that all by yourself for so long after I left."

Kylie surged up to kiss him softly. "You don't need to apologize at all. As far as I'm concerned, we dodged a pretty big bullet there. The way my luck's been going lately, I would have definitely gotten pregnant."

"Doesn't mean I shouldn't feel rotten about it. Should we be worried about your father showing up here?"

"If I don't call him soon, he'll definitely be pounding on my apartment door so hard that we'd hear him up here before morning. I couldn't completely hide how god-awful I felt from my voice so he could tell something was up. I lied and told him I thought I had the stomach flu. He sent my friend, Molly, over with some medicine, and I was supposed to call him before she left. Then Jennifer showed up just as Molly was leaving, and I was so busy trying to explain who she was without giving anything away that I completely forgot. I left my cell phone in the bag he sent over."

"You can use mine," he offered.

Kylie shook her head. "He'd freak if I did. He doesn't know about you or any of this, remember? Plus, I'm supposed to be sick in bed trying not to puke my guts up."

She reluctantly pulled herself away from his warmth and sat back on her haunches beside him. "I need to go get the change of clothes he sent over, anyway. In the meantime, can I borrow a t-shirt and a pair of sweat-pants or something?"

Hunter snorted. "You'll look like a kid playing dress-up in her father's clothes." His eyes traveled down the length of her body that was now on full display before he gave himself a hard shake and sat up as well. "Let me get it for you. I imagine you're probably feeling pretty sore right now."

Kylie had felt a momentary panic before she forced herself to give him a sour look. There was no way she could let him anywhere near that bag while the bracelet and Paul's toothbrush were still inside, so she couldn't afford for him to get suspicious now.

"Exactly," she huffed. "That's why there's no way I'm letting you go anywhere *near* that apartment and its pheromones of doom! As delicious as you look right now, I really don't think my body can handle that monster again tonight!"

He grinned, looking entirely too smug for her peace of mind. "Don't worry. The beauty of being a shifter is that we recover fast."

Kylie fingered the tender place on her collarbone that likely sported Hunter's teeth marks. Yeah, she definitely didn't want Paul seeing the wound. She needed time to figure out how to explain to him why she had decided to get involved with Hunter at such a dangerous time that didn't involve the words "hot body."

"Great. Now, if you're finished looking like the

Cheshire Cat's sexy cousin, I'm going to dig in your closet for a shirt."

"It might be best if I put some clothes on, too," Hunter said, getting up and following her somewhat stilted gait across the room to the closet. "Pheromones or not, it'll be hard to resist you once you come back to bed if I'm still naked."

"You're insatiable," Kylie scolded, though she wasn't irritated in the least. Just thinking about all the wild and passionate sex they had just had sent a flair of heat into her sex that had her squeezing her legs together.

After throwing on a white t-shirt and a pair of black sweatpants that she was practically swimming in even after rolling up the cuffs and cinching the drawstring, Kylie spent a good five minutes being kissed enthusiastically by her new lover before he allowed her to leave the bedroom. She returned to the bathroom to retrieve her apartment key from her discarded jeans and barefoot, hurried down to her new apartment before anyone could see her in that ridiculous getup.

Once inside, Kylie wasted no time in grabbing the gym bag and then shutting herself into the foyer closet. Hopefully, the pheromones still circulating in the air were minimal inside. At any rate, she would only be there for a few minutes tops. Any longer, and Hunter might decide to come see what was taking her so long.

She plopped her butt onto the ground and dug out her cell phone. She was relieved when Paul picked up after the first ring.

"Kylie! Thank God!" Paul exclaimed before she could breathe a word. "It's almost one! When you didn't call even an hour after Molly left the hospital to take you the things you asked for and you didn't answer your phone, I thought for sure the toothbrush hadn't worked, and something awful had happened to you!"

"Where are you now?" Kylie asked.

"On my way to the ER nurse's station. I was about to ask Karen to go look in on you..."

"No! Don't do that!" Kylie said frantically. "Hunter doesn't know that we're friends with a cougar yet. He sent an elementary school teacher from the jaguar clan named Jennifer Graham to sit with me all night. She stepped out for a moment to talk to Hunter at his apartment, but she'll be back any minute. We have to keep this call short."

"You need to somehow get the Elders to agree to allow you to reveal yourself as a shifter to me soon, or things will get very tedious rather quickly," he warned. "But never mind that for now. You sound normal, so I take it the items worked?"

"Thankfully, yes. Once everything settles down here,

I'll come see you to explain in more detail. I'll tell Hunter that we have a lunch date again on Sunday."

"I hate to say this, but I'm glad Hunter is looking after you so closely," Paul said. "Karen says that someone else in her clan has seen a couple of unknown shifters that she feels have been behaving suspiciously enough to possibly be Sniffers. We may not yet know the jaguars' plans for you, but at least I know the last thing they would want is for you to be harmed or the lions to get a hold of you."

"Don't worry. After this whole heat-cycle nightmare tonight, I doubt Hunter will let me out of his sight for the next few days. This will be a good opportunity to try to weasel some info from him about the lions. He accidentally brought them up today, so naturally, I jumped at the chance to ask questions."

"Anything new?" Paul asked hopefully.

"No, but from some of the evasive answers he was giving me, I'm almost positive that he knows more."

"Just be careful, Kylie, and please, please don't let your guard down with Hunter. Karen told me that he doesn't have a mate or even a prospective mate. He may be after something much more practical than searching out the identities of your parents."

Yes, and he got it and then some, Kylie thought ruefully.

Paul really was going to be pissed with her when she finally found the guts to tell him.

"Always," she promised. "You make sure to take care of yourself, too, and I'll see you on Sunday."

More Sniffers… Kylie suddenly realized that she had never gotten a straight answer from Hunter about whether or not he knew of any Sniffers currently skulking around Riverford. He had managed to completely distract her, damn him—though she had to admit that she was also partially to blame for allowing one measly smile to waylay her. However, that didn't change the fact that he had heavily implied that there were. There could be more Sniffers roaming the city than any of them had ever guessed. The thought was terrifying.

Hunter was waiting for her in his living room, still dressed in the t-shirt and boxers he had slipped on, and casually sprawled out on the couch with a rather peaceful expression. However, when she approached, his nostrils flared, and his eyes zeroed onto the gym bag.

Kylie had been counting on this reaction. "That bad, huh? I was afraid of that. The clothes inside should be okay, but do you have a trash bag I can put this in until I can wash it? I'd throw it out, but it's my dad's."

"Under the sink," Hunter replied in a strained voice, obviously trying not to breathe.

Kylie hurried over to the kitchen and located a box of black, heavy duty trash bags. She pulled out everything in the gym bag except for the white paper sack and its secrets, placing the clothing on the counter before securing it inside the large trash bag.

The whole time, she could feel Hunter's eyes on her back. It made the jaguar within bristle. Having your back to a predator, even if that predator was your lover, was never comfortable.

"Put it in the guest room just to be safe," Hunter instructed once she turned around, his voice just a tad bit deeper than usual. "I'll wait for you in the bedroom."

A wave of arousal washed through her at his words even though she knew he probably hadn't meant them to be suggestive. She sighed. Her entire body was still incredibly sore both inside and out, so no matter how hot she was getting for him, her body needed to rest.

She put the bag inside the closet in the guest room just for a little more added peace of mind before climbing back into bed with Hunter, his arms enveloping her into a warm, fragrant cocoon of jaguar maleness as she snuggled up to his chest. Who would have thought after the hellish way the night had begun that it would end on such a fantastic note?

Hunter kissed the top of her head tenderly. "Try to get some sleep. We'll patrol my territory together tomorrow morning. It's about time I took you on that run I promised."

"It's a date," Kylie replied, and then added amusedly, "just as long as the date doesn't end with you bringing me a dead rabbit for lunch instead of taking me to a restaurant."

A snort was his only reply.

CHAPTER 23

The eastern horizon had barely begun to lighten as Hunter and Kylie walked hand-in-hand into the forest behind Hunter's apartment complex.

"When you said a morning run, I was expecting a bit more light," Kylie teased with a yawn.

Although she had already witnessed the incredible healing speed of a shifter body, Kylie was still impressed that even the teeth marks on her shoulder were gone, replaced by a faint purple bruise that would probably disappear completely by the afternoon. They had even been able to enjoy a bit of bed play before getting ready to head out into the forest.

Without Kylie's pheromones to enflame him beyond reason, Hunter had opted for a more leisurely rhythm that was less urgency and more worship that had Kylie screaming nonetheless. Even now, her nipples still felt a bit sore from the attentions of his talented mouth.

"There will be, once you shift," Hunter said with a grin.

"Right. I forgot jaguars can see really good in the dark. How much of this is your territory?" Kylie asked.

"About twenty square miles."

"Really? So much?"

"It hasn't always been mine. Some of it belongs to my family."

"That's right. You did mention a brother before."

When the hand gripping her own tensed, Kylie hastily added, "Sorry. You don't have to say anything else about him if you don't want."

Hunter was quiet for a long moment as they walked farther into the trees before he sighed and squeezed her hand. "When we know each other a little better, then I'll tell you about him sometime."

"Okay," was all she could think to reply.

She couldn't help but wonder if his brother was even still alive. Of course, a falling out could often be equally as painful, especially if they had been extremely close.

Grasping for something to distract him from the melancholia that had fallen over him, Kylie asked, "How much farther is the cave you mentioned?"

Hunter flashed her a grateful smile. "Not much farther. That it's so close to the forest's edge is the reason I use it to store my clothes while I'm shifted. It's so small that it's not good for much else. Oh, and before I forget, once you're shifted, be on the lookout for humans. Sometimes one or two'll wander pretty deep into the forest and just happen to catch a glimpse of us while we're shifted. That's why there're so many stories of people seeing jaguars around here when there haven't been any of the non-shifter variety living in the wild here in Texas for decades."

"Not just jaguars, but I've heard stories of 'black panther' sightings all over the state, too," Kylie said with a nod.

Hunter laughed. "Yeah, about that, I don't know if you've ever met Ed Betancourt—he's a plumber—but all those sightings come courtesy of his cousin Charlie who lives in California. Charlie's jaguar is melanistic, and he enjoys popping up on unsuspecting people while on his runs. He's proud to have added to the local legends of several states."

"Yeah, it's all fun and games until someone shoots him," Kylie replied dryly.

"Oh, they already have," Hunter said, not looking particularly concerned. "We don't have any melanistics in our clan, but we do have someone whose jaguar is an albino with blue eyes. I'll introduce you to him sometime. Like Charlie, he enjoys showing himself off, though he's nowhere near as obnoxious about it."

"Speaking of, I hope everyone I was supposed to meet yesterday isn't too irritated that we never showed."

"Kylie—I hate to break it to you, but I think *every* shifter in Riverford has heard about you unleashing the full potency of your charms in Southern Glacier by now."

"College on Monday is going to be sheer torture, isn't it?" she moaned. "I hate being the center of attention on the best of days, and now I have to worry about people snickering behind my back. Only two days as a shifter and I've already managed to make myself a laughingstock!"

Hunter rubbed a thumb soothingly over her hand. "You said your major was biology, right?"

"Yeah. Pre-med like my dad, though I was thinking of maybe changing from biology to genetics. Rather than be a family doctor, I'd be interested in developing gene therapies for all those nasty genetic disorders."

Hunter suddenly stopped cold. "Genetics is often a career path lion shifters choose," he said slowly. "In fact, most of the top geneticists in the world are lion shifters. They're also really big in pharmaceuticals. Going into that kind of field—well, let's just say it tends to make the clans really suspicious."

Yes, I know. Kylie had gotten exactly the kind of response she had hoped for. Unfortunately, the timing of his question sucked. This was hardly the place or the time to try to dig more information out of him, especially when he said that they were supposed to be patrolling for Sniffers and trespassing gator shifters. Yet…

He may now be her lover, but that didn't mean she wasn't going to be relentless in pursuing any and everything he knew about the lion clans. Damn. She would just have to get what she could now and find a way to bring the subject up later on tonight.

She had made her choice last night when she had taken Hunter's face into her hands and crossed the line that shouldn't have been crossed, and that meant leaving Riverford was no longer an option. She couldn't afford to falter now that she had so much more to lose.

"Are you trying to tell me that studying genetics is— what? *Taboo?*" Kylie demanded with as much outrage as she could muster.

He sighed and looked at her with dismay. "Taboo doesn't even begin to describe it. It's as good as announcing yourself as a lion supporter."

"Well, there goes that career out the window," Kylie

spat. "It's a good thing I'm still just a junior and not very far along into the core curriculum yet. At least tell me that other medical fields are okay, or I think I might just start spitting fire!"

"Just stay away from genetics and pharmacology, and you'll be good. Leave the fire spitting to the dragon shifters."

"Wait—what? *Dragon shifters!*" Kylie exclaimed in genuine shock. There's no way there could be—her parents would have definitely told—

"Dammit! You're pulling my leg, aren't you?" she accused just as he exploded into laughter.

Hunter pulled her against his chest and planted a firm kiss on her lips. "The look on your face was priceless. The closest we come to dragons are the komodo shifters, though if I had to pick a clan other than jaguar, I wouldn't have minded being born the mythological type of dragon shifter."

Kylie scowled. "I'm so glad my ignorance amuses you. We'll see how much you're laughing tonight when I go stay at my dad's instead of your place."

"Maybe I should call you my little firecat instead of hellcat," he said with a grin, not looking concerned at all by her threat.

"And maybe I should just knee you in the—"

Kylie abruptly turned her head sharply to the right

and scented the air a split-second before Hunter did the same, her jaguar senses going into full warning mode. As the wind had slightly shifted, three new smells had entered her sphere of awareness all at once. She had smelled all of them before, one just last night coming from Hunter's tiger friend Maxim's security guards. Another was an acrid smell that tickled her memory but wasn't immediately evident. However the last—there was no mistaking *that* coppery scent.

Blood.

CHAPTER 24

The look in Hunter's eyes was one hundred percent jaguar, deadly and inhuman, as he stared off into the darkness of the forest in the direction where the stench of blood was strongest. A low, menacing growl rose from his throat, and it took everything Kylie had in her to keep herself from growling, too. Something told her it would just set Hunter even more on edge. If there was danger, she didn't want him getting hurt over some shifter instinct to protect his female.

"It's a male wolf shifter," he said, his lips pressing together tightly into a hard line, "about a couple hundred yards deeper."

He turned to look down at her, and the threat in his eyes softened to something that just looked troubled.

"Damn it—I need to go check things out, but I can't let you go back to the apartment alone. You can smell it, can't you? The blood? The fear?"

Kylie suddenly stilled. An image of the sick bastard that had attacked her covered in blood from her claws flashed into her mind. It was no wonder that the acrid smell was familiar. She had smelled enough fear that horrible night to last her a lifetime.

Her heart sped up. "Is he alone?" she asked softly, taking a deeper whiff of the air.

It smelled like only one individual's scent, but she was still too new to her shifter nature to trust her judgment just yet.

Hunter glanced back into the forest before he fixed her with an even more troubled look. "I don't smell any scent other than the wolf's and my own territory markings, but..." He released her and grabbed her right hand tightly. "Come on. Stay at my back, and no matter what happens, if I tell you to shift and run, *you do it.*"

"What's going on, Hunter?" Kylie demanded as they hurried towards the wolf.

"Ignoring the fact that a wolf entered my territory without permission, there's no way someone that's lost the amount of blood I smell could have come this far alone without help," Hunter replied darkly. "So, unless he came out here to commit suicide, he had to have been either dumped in here to die, or he was injured here. Hate to say it, but I'm hoping it's a suicide."

"What! *Why?*" Kylie exclaimed, completely taken aback.

Hunter glanced over his shoulder at her. "Because if someone else entered this forest with him, then they managed to *completely mask their scent.* Hell, even rocks have a scent. Only someone wearing a hazmat suit can do that, and I don't imagine that type of protective gear is something you'd readily find outside of a lab or a Prepper's doomsday bunker. Remember what I told you about the lions? That they were geneticists?"

Kylie felt her blood run cold. "You think—how sure are you that it's them?"

"All I can say is that the lions have breached other shifter territories using hazmats before," he replied grimly.

Kylie squeezed his hand in alarm. "Then that means they could still be in your territory somewhere!"

Her eyes darted nervously to the vast gulf of trees that surrounded them. The sun had risen a little bit farther over the horizon, but it was still too dark for her human eyes to see any detail beyond basic shapes.

"Or we could both be jumping at shadows," he added with a small, self-deprecating smile.

The snap of a twig had Hunter suddenly crouching

down into a defensive stance in front of her with a hiss. The sound was so cliché that for a moment, Kylie had to struggle not to start giggling like a loon. Then movement in the far-off gloom caught her eye, and she instantly lost all desire to laugh, to even *breathe*.

For an endless moment, all Kylie could hear was the thumping of her racing heart and the rattling of tree branches in the wind as she stared hard at the trees. The rest of the forest had gone unnaturally silent.

Here there be predators...

Then she heard it, a faint, high-pitched whine like that of a dog on its last breath. Unconsciously, Kylie leaned forward and squinted in the direction of that sound before recoiling as her nose was abruptly inundated with the metallic smell of blood a split-second before a reddish, tawny-colored wolf head popped out from behind the large trunk of a tree only a few feet away. Kylie let out a short cry of startlement and backpeddled a couple of steps before she saw the wolf head suddenly collapse onto its side.

Without a word, Hunter straightened, and Kylie found herself being tugged by the hand behind him as her lover hurried over to the fallen animal. She could hear the wolf's labored breathing before they had even reached him.

When the wolf's entire body came into view, Kylie let

out another cry, but this time it was one of horror. Even in the barely-there light of early morning, Kylie could clearly see all the blood without her nose practically screaming it into her brain. The fur of his back and legs was so matted with blood that the wolf almost appeared as though he had been partially skinned.

"My God..."

Bile rose to Kylie's throat as she let go of Hunter's hand and dropped to her knees beside the poor creature, wanting to help him with everything in her being but unsure how or even if he *could* be helped at this point.

The wolf's eyes were closed tightly, its muzzle a rictus of unimaginable pain. He was still breathing, but the ragged breaths were now almost inaudible.

"What can we do?" Kylie asked faintly as Hunter knelt down beside her. With that much blood, it was dangerous for her to get any nearer.

"I'll call Needles, but..." He trailed off, but he didn't need to finish.

Hunter dug out his cell phone from his front pocket while Kylie placed a hand gently onto the wolf's head in a gesture of comfort. It was one of the few uninjured places on his mutilated body. She wanted to let him know that at least he wasn't alone, that someone was horrified at what had been done to him.

This close, the smell of blood was so strong it was

nauseating. In order to distract herself from it, Kylie tried focusing on Hunter's voice as he spoke urgently into his phone, but it was as though the smell had permanently stained the inside of her nostrils. She imagined she would now smell it for days.

"He dragged himself."

Kylie jumped at the sudden declaration at her ear before she turned slightly to look at the place Hunter pointed towards. A trail of blood, disturbed dead leaves, and squashed grass led through the trees straight to the pitiful body before her.

Kylie swallowed thickly. "That he even managed to move at all is mindboggling. There's so much blood, I can't even tell how he's injured!"

"We need to try to get him to wake up," Hunter said. "He needs to shift back into his human form to have any hope of surviving long enough for Needles and his crew to get here."

The poor guy had probably passed out from the pain. It seemed cruel to have to wake him, but Kylie just nodded and bent down to his ear. However, before Kylie could say a word, the wolf's muscles seemed to ripple all at once, causing her to flinch back with her heart suddenly in her throat. He let out a pained howl before he began to rapidly shift back into a man.

The wounds on his back had become more visible as

the fur was replaced with skin. Wide, gaping lines of sliced-open skin and muscle were pulled wider open until she could have laid her entire arm lengthwise within some of them. Then in the next second, they stretched out into slices the width of a pencil and as long as the length of his back from shoulder to just shy of his butt. As he shifted, the wolf shifter's howls of agony gradually turned into the screams of a man.

The entire process had happened in less than a minute, but it was one of the most horrifying things Kylie had ever seen, and as she had often found herself in the ER many an evening to see Paul, she'd seen a damn lot—including wounds very similar to this.

"Those are claw marks, aren't they?" Kylie exclaimed. "His entire back is shredded just like a guy I once saw in the ER that was attacked by a leopard he was keeping illegally as a pet inside his house."

"Yes," the wolf shifter answered hoarsely.

Her eyes instantly flew back down to the bleeding man's face and met a pair of pale, pain-filled eyes.

"Don't try to talk," she said firmly. "Hunter's called for help. Just stay still and save your strength."

"Hunter!" The wolf abruptly grabbed Hunter's arm, making Kylie yelp in surprise. "Thank God I found you!" he slurred. "My mate! You have to save my mate—*please*! He said you could help us—all of us!"

"Whoa, slow down, buddy. What the hell happened to you?" Hunter demanded. "Who said I could help you?"

"Your brother," he gasped, and then promptly passed out.

"His brother?" Kylie echoed, turning questionably to Hunter—and gasped.

Hunter looked for all the world like he had just been kicked in the face by a horse.

CHAPTER 25

"Hunter?" Kylie said hesitantly, reaching out a hand to him, but unsure if she should touch him.

At the sound of her voice, utter shock quickly turned to a frenzy of activity as Hunter yanked off his fleece jacket, followed by the long-sleeved Henley he wore, leaving his chest bare. He then proceeded to tear it apart at the seams before handing her the back piece.

"We need to try to stop the bleeding," he said, his voice thick with urgency. "Even if he screams, don't stop putting pressure on the wounds."

Kylie wanted to question him about the wolf's words. It was obvious that just mentioning his brother had shaken Hunter to the core. Instead, she just nodded, folded the fabric into a makeshift compress, and silently set about to carefully apply pressure to the worst of the gaping slashes on the wolf shifter's lower back that were still oozing blood. There were so many of them that it looked as though a monster cat had decided to use his back as a scratching post. She had no idea how he was still alive.

The entire time, her heart was racing in a new fear. She was too close to the blood, dangerously close. It was quickly soaking through the layers she had folded into the cotton fabric, but thankfully had yet to penetrate the outside layer. The wounded man wasn't human, so if so much as a drop got on her skin...

"The lions did this," she stated, not daring to take her eyes off her hands.

For a long, uncomfortable moment, Hunter didn't answer. Kylie could almost physically feel the gears in his head turning as he considered her words.

"The fact that he mentioned my brother guarantees it," Hunter said finally, the reluctance still evident in his tone.

Startled, Kylie chanced a glance at him and was surprised to see him staring intently into the trees towards the south with his teeth clenched as if he was seconds away from snarling. She instantly stiffened, wondering if he had seen or heard something just now.

She couldn't smell anything but blood and more blood, and to a lesser extent, the scent of wolf and jaguar.

"Hunter, wha—"

Without warning, Hunter shoved her shoulder hard with both hands, sending her tumbling, as a large, golden mass landed directly onto his back from somewhere above. A blood-curdling roar shattered the silence behind her, and Kylie froze in the middle of trying to right herself for a couple of heartbeats before an answering growl rose from her throat.

Fueled by a surge of adrenaline, Kylie rolled and scrambled to her knees. She raised her head in enough time to see a cougar—no, a *lioness*—go flying as Hunter, pinned flat on his back and dangerously close to having his throat ripped out, shoved the lioness off him with a brutal upward kick of his heavy boots to her midsection. She was horrified to see a deep, double gash in his forearm as though the lioness had bitten down and tried to tear a chunk out of the muscle. He also had a few shallow slashes across his chest where he had been clawed.

"Shift and run! *Now!*" Hunter yelled a heartbeat before he began to shift himself, his jeans ripping as his body began to rapidly contort and reshape itself.

Then the lioness was on him again, and the morning air was suddenly filled with the roars and snarls of two apex cats as they locked together in a mass of snapping jaws and razor sharp claws.

Kylie sat a few feet away from the melee frozen in both horror and indecision. Although Hunter was the larger of the two, the lioness seemed to have the upper hand, her movements more deliberate and precise —trained.

Dammit! Although scared out of her mind, she knew she couldn't just run off and leave Hunter and the dying wolf to the mercy of that monster. She started to take off the jacket Hunter had loaned her when suddenly six hundred plus pounds of tumbling cats came flying at her. Kylie yelped and tried to dive out of the way, but the back end of the lioness clipped her right side painfully hard, knocking her to the ground.

Gasping for a breath that was no longer there, Kylie tried to pick herself off the ground for the second time that day. Through tearing eyes, she saw the battling felines slam into a thick tree trunk dangerously close to the unconscious wolf shifter.

Shaking his head rapidly and obviously stunned, Hunter staggered over to the wolf, placing himself as a barrier between the wolf and the lioness, who had abruptly switched her attack back to the person who had been her target all along. There was a meaty sound as their bodies collided, but this time, as they tumbled to the ground in a tangle of limbs, only the lioness climbed back to her feet.

Kylie's muscles throughout her body were already contracting as she opened her mouth to scream at the lioness, a scream initially meant to distract that quickly turned into a roar of pure rage that sounded unlike anything she had ever heard come out of her mouth. The lioness pivoted with a snarl, then froze with a look of confusion that had no business on the face of a lion.

Taking advantage of the enemy shifter's bewilderment, Kylie shot straight for the bitch and lunged for her throat. Her jaws, however, met only air as the lioness somehow managed to twist out of the way at the last second. Kylie immediately turned and crouched low with a snarl, prepared to defend both her knocked-out lover and the injured wolf shifter no matter what.

However, instead of attacking, the lioness gave a low grunt and slowly sat back onto her haunches. Then the muscles of her body began to ripple, and Kylie was utterly staggered when she realized that the lioness was *shifting*. Another thirty seconds and a short-haired, blonde woman crouched in the lioness's place, glaring fit to kill.

"What the hell is a lioness doing with the *jaguars?*" the woman angrily demanded in an alto voice the second she was able, spitting out the word 'jaguar' like an expletive. Her nostrils flared. "I can smell him all over you! It's so strong that I thought you were one of them! That you would shame your Alpha, your clan, by letting that piece of filth fuck you is just...!" She growled in utter disgust. "Traitor!"

Lioness...

If Kylie had been in her human form, all of her blood would have drained from her face in utter dread. She slowly lowered her eyes, the look on her face like someone expecting to see something gory and grotesque. As soon as two golden paws that were conspicuously free of spots came into view, Kylie jerked her eyes away. She'd seen more than enough.

The blonde woman's eyes flickered to a point behind Kylie before she growled again, turned and dashed into the cover of the trees without another word. With the threat gone for the moment, Kylie wasted no time in shifting back to her human form.

"You're—a Polyshifter."

Kylie flinched at the utter flatness in the familiar voice behind her, at hearing a word she hated almost as much as the word 'Deadend.' It was a word that had the power to destroy, and already had destroyed, a multitude of lives. It was the hated label that had cost Kylie her parents.

For one desperate moment, she considered just

dashing off into the trees, and then almost in the same thought, berated herself disgustedly for even thinking it. She owed it to Hunter to stay. She owed it to herself. She had to see what, if any, expression was on his face; she had to *know*...

She slowly stood up, turned, and faced him with her nudity fully on display. And there it was, one of her worst fears staring back at her in the form of a pair of hazel eyes full of suspicion and the first hints of betrayal.

In that endless, horrible moment, there were only two paths Kylie could see. Her days of feigning ignorance about the shifter world were now irrevocably over.

She could either shift back into a lioness and run to Paul and a life forever on the run, essentially ruining the life of a man who had taken her in without batting an eye and given her everything, or she could come completely clean and try to salvage the best thing that had ever happened to her no matter how impossible it now seemed.

"I am," Kylie confessed softly, refusing to look away.

It was done. The next move was completely his.

ACCEPTING THE JAGUAR

RIVERFORD SHIFTERS BOOK TWO

Kylie knew from the beginning that getting romantically involved with Hunter was an extremely bad idea, and now because of the Pandora's Box she inadvertently blew wide open in order to protect him, more than just Hunter may now determine the consequences she and those she loves will ultimately end up paying.

NOW AVAILABLE!

ABOUT THE AUTHOR

Cristina Rayne is a *New York Times* and *USA Today* best-selling author who lives in West Texas with her crazy cat and about a dozen bookcases full of fantasy worlds and steamy romances. She has a degree in Computer Science which totally qualifies her to write romances. As Fantasy is her first love, she feels if she can inject a little love into the fantastical, along with a few steamy scenes, then all the better. She is the author of the *Elven King, The Elven Realms, Riverford Shifters, Dragon Shifters of Elysia, Incarnations of Myth, The Vampire Underground* paranormal romance series, and the *Fractured Multiverse* science-fantasy series.

www.cristinarayneauthor.com

facebook.com/CristinaRayneAuthor

twitter.com/CRayneAuthor

amazon.com/author/cristinarayne

goodreads.com/Cristina_Rayne